Salem's Fury

Vengeance Trilogy: Book Two

Aaron Galvin

Aames & Abernathy Publishing

Salem's Fury
Vengeance Trilogy: Book Two

Published by Aames & Abernathy Publishing,
Chino Hills, CA USA

Edited by Annetta Ribken.
You can find her at *www.wordwebbing.com*
Copy Edits by Jennifer Wingard.
www.theindependentpen.com
Cover Design by Greg Sidelnik.
www.gregsidelnik.com
Book design and formatting by Valerie Bellamy.
www.dog-earbookdesign.com
Cover photo by villorejo/Shutterstock

ISBN-10: 150894251X
ISBN-13: 978-1508942511

Printed in the USA

Also by Aaron Galvin

Salted
Salt Series: Book I

Taken With A Grain of Salt
Salt Series: Book II

Salem's Vengeance
Vengeance Trilogy: Book I

Find out more about Aaron Galvin:
Website: *www.aarongalvin.com*

for my daughters

&

to Martha & Abel

Thank you for reading my books! :)

C Gl

-one-

- October, 1727 -
Miamiak Territory

My freedom hails with the wild.

Today, it finds me riding a birch-bark canoe down the river my people name Wah-Bah-Shik-Ka, the water over white stones.

"Girl!"

I ignore the taunt from the neighboring canoe.

"Rebecca!"

Like the braves in our tribe, the boy who calls my attention bears the tattoos of our people upon his chest, arms, and face—all of them marking him for a Miamiak tribesman.

But Ciquenackqua is no brave yet.

"I see no girl among us," I say to him. "Only hunters. And one boy."

My response draws laughter from our menfolk. The boy's face reddens.

"My father and I would race you and Deep River to the beaver dam," he says.

I look ahead, gathering the distance and watching the head of our canoe dip and rise with the current.

"What say you, girl?" Ciquenackqua asks me. "We brought many pelts for the trade, but I would gladly take half of yours as winnings."

I glance to the seat behind me where sits my friend, Deep River. He signals he will follow my lead.

"And if you lose, Ciquenackqua?" I ask the boy. "What then?"

"The son of Whistling Hare does not lose," he says.

Our shaman, Creek Jumper, announces the race to cheers from the menfolk. I clutch my oar tight when he signals our start with a war cry.

The front position grants me the best view of our race and, for a time, the tips of our canoe and Ciquenackqua's pace one another.

I glance over and observe Ciquenackqua's confidence. He crows when they pull ahead.

At my whistle, Deep River and I dip our oars low into the water, near to the hilt, coaxing more speed with powerful strokes.

Our canoe pulls ahead.

Ciquenackqua paddles quick and shallow.

"Deeper, son!" His father roars. "The river rewards skill, not panic."

I tune out their voices, losing myself to the twin sounds of my oar paddling in unison with my partner's as we pull away.

Deep River and I pass the dam first. Along with more cheers from the men, a smack echoes behind us. I think it a beaver, slapping its tail, at first, but it is only Ciquenackqua striking his oar upon the water.

I think to laugh at him, yet keep my silence in humble victory.

Ciquenackqua says little the remainder of the morning, though our party offers me congratulations.

My excitement blooms near noon when we drift around the

familiar river bend. Smoke rises from the chimneys of several cabins. A few wagons sit next to a barn. Horses whinny, and cows and sheep graze together. Two men work beside a stack of timber, the pair of them sawing back and forth through a felled tree.

A pack of dogs bark and alert both men to our presence.

I recognize my brother's build even before he turns.

Our sister, Sarah, often says her god made George in the same mold as our father. Broad-shouldered and taller than any brave, he bears the look of a woodland man, his face bearded and full, body hardened by the days spent lumbering in the wilderness and attending the many tasks his trade post demands.

George drops his end of the saw and whistles. His wife, Hannah, emerges from the largest cabin, wiping her hands on her apron, and hurries to join him.

The sight of both coming down the hill to greet us makes me eager to reach the shore first.

George wades into the water, lifts his hand in acknowledgment.

The moment we close on him, I leap from our canoe and into his arms, my weight knocking him backward. Enveloped by the frigid water, my body questions the sanity of such an act. It vanishes when I rise for air and hear my brother's laughter. He drenches me anew by placing his worn, floppy hat upon my head.

"You've grown, little sister," George says.

"And you," I say. "But not wiser, I see."

He dunks me again.

I rise from the water sputtering. My attempt at dunking him again fails when he throws me over his shoulder. I rise to his laughter.

"Care to try again?" George asks.

"No," I say. "Peace between us…for now."

We wade back to shore, but my brother keeps his distance, too smart to fall for my ruse.

"Rebecca!" Hannah embraces me, heedless of my wet buckskin breeches and top. "We hoped Priest would bring you when next he came."

George barks a laugh. "Had he ordered her to stay, no doubt she would have discovered a means of arriving first."

"My brother knows me well," I say. "Perhaps as well as Father."

George's face sours a bit at my naming Priest as Father. Yet, unlike our sister, he speaks naught of it. Instead, he watches the many braves beaching their canoes alongside mine, squinting at each canoe beached.

"Where is Priest?" he asks.

"Home," I say. "Gathering more skins for you to trade."

George frowns. "Keeping peace with our sister you mean."

"Come now, husband." Hannah places her arm through the crook of his. "What good is a husband if he does not keep his wife happy?"

"Aye," says George. "But I should like to have spoken with him."

"What of?"

My brother's jaw clenches at my question.

"I hear rumor of rogue war parties ranging further west." He sighs. "Some say the Iroquois will be upon our doorstep before long."

"Must you always be so dour, good husband?" says Hannah. "Your guests and sister have only just arrived. Let you attend them now. And pleasantly."

My brother's smile draws one from me also. He goes from man to man, calling each by name, shaking their hands, jesting with them.

In my soul, I wish that Sarah had come. I know it would do her well to witness our brother prosperous and happy. His post be a three-day journey by river though, and Sarah has oft claimed her body cannot bear the land route home.

I turn my attention up the hill where Andrew Martin watches us. He does not come down, even when I raise my hand to him.

He walks into the barn, never acknowledging me.

I find the ill will he yet bears me unsettling, and wonder if I might alter his negative view or if I should bother in the attempt.

"He will be at this all day now." Hannah chuckles and points to my brother.

"Aye," I say. "He has a mind for the trade."

"Indeed," she says to me. "Will you help me with the cooking, sister?"

"Aye. But first I would meet with the old bear."

"He will be most happy to see you," Hannah says. "Today has been among the better in a long while for him. No doubt your presence will cheer him further."

She takes my arm in hers as we journey up the hill, leaving the men to talk and trade. One of the older dogs follows us, licking at my hand along the walk. We pass a smokehouse, a carpentry shed, and even a newly built trade cabin, full of goods—powder and shot, cloth, whiskey, and the like.

"You have prospered much since my last visit," I say upon weaving around the side of one cabin.

"Aye," says Hannah. "I swear God made it that your brother

requires no sleep. He works at the post day and night, come rain or snow. Always he finds something to set his hand to."

I look on the new constructions again and shake my head. "But he and Andrew could not have done this alone."

"No," she says. "The last winter's snow forced not a few French traders to shelter among us. They repaid their debt by aiding us build and helping grow the post as partners. One yet remains with his wife, Mary. A shy creature, she is, but female company I have been most fortunate to have among all these men."

I laugh. "No doubt my brother is happy as well then."

"Aye," Hannah says. "It saddens me Mary leaves soon. Her husband's partners journeyed south in the spring to build another post. They recently sent word back all is prepared for Jacque and Mary to join them in time for winter. Would that word had not come until spring."

Her tone beckons me think on Sarah, alone in our hut. My thoughts return to the good it would have done her spirit to visit, perhaps even winter with George and Hannah, and I remind myself to insist Sarah think on it upon my return.

We stop in front of a cabin I well remember, the first build of the post. Small traps that some might believe laid for rodents clutter outside its door and yard.

The sight reminds me of the many days I spent checking each trap in my youth. No small part of me yet wishes to discover a leprechaun and present the devious creature to the equally devious man who taught me of them.

"I shall leave you to him," Hannah says, drawing her arm from mine. "My presence would only draw his ire."

"Why?"

She frowns. "His mind wanders more each passing season.

Most days he asks if I am a banshee, come to sing the final song and take him home. Others he runs me off, naming me a witch desiring to poison him with Devil's powder."

I laugh at imagining him in just such a way, and harder still when I question whether Bishop's wits have truly left him, or if he does all for show. A trick pleasing to himself, no doubt, and one I know from which he takes great enjoyment.

Hannah pats my hand before taking her leave of me.

I step to the porch and knock on the door, hardly able to contain my excitement.

Receiving no answer, I knock again.

"Grandfather," I call.

When no answer comes, I try the latch and discover it barred.

"Grandfather. It is I, your favored one, Rebecca."

A third time I knock upon the door, harder.

Fear swells in my gut as I leave the door to peer through the open window.

My eyes settle on a lumpy figure, lain on the floor near the hearth, his body covered by a bearskin, his hand outstretched, unmoving.

"Grandfather!"

I crawl through the window and tumble into the room. Hurrying to Bishop's side, I pull back the bearskin hide from his face.

The years have turned his once dark and grey hair near all white, while discolored blotches mar his wrinkled skin. He wheezes as I roll him to his back, and his unscarred right eye flutters open.

"Are ye the banshee?" Bishop asks me, his voice weak and withered. "Come at last to sing me home?"

"No..."

"Hmm. Thought not. Too pretty." He groans as he sits up then hacks up phlegm and spits it into a chamber pot. "No. An old hag and ugly to boot, that's the sort of banshee I'd have come for me. A wailin' bitch to fright these bones awake. Make me fight for life."

"I do not doubt you will fight to the end," I say.

Bishop coughs in a grievous fit I like not at all, hacking more phlegm the color of earth. He looks around the room as one lost to his surroundings then glances at me. "How did I end up on the floor, then?"

I shake my head. "I only just arrived and found you here."

"Ah. Me damned legs gave out on me again, I'll warrant." He struggles to stand, leaning heavy on a tipped chair. "That or one of the little people tripped me and stole me wits away. They prey on old folk, or so me father claimed once."

I help him to a bench beside his table and attempt to guide him down.

He sits harder than I like, wincing upon his landing. "I'll get me one o' the wee bastards yet though, lass. Squeeze me three wishes out of him, I would."

"What would you wish for?"

He perks at my question, his bushy eyebrows rising. "Me first would be that the little man exile me to the isle o' Pago-Pago."

"The island where only women live," I say.

"Told you before, eh?"

"Aye," I say. "Many times over, but I would hear it again gladly. What good would you do there?"

"Ah, nuthin' good, lass," he says. "And that be the reason for me second wish—to make me a young man again so

I could chase them women 'round me island and they could ne'er escape me."

"You would not wish for your wife to live again?"

Bishop waves me off. "I've the rest of eternity to hear me poor Annie blather on. Why not enjoy meself a bit o' peace and quiet yet?"

I chuckle at the familiar stories. "And the third wish?"

"Augh," he says. "Ye know I can't be tellin' ye that, lass. An old man's gotta save off some secrets to hisself, else there'd be nuthin' to keep a pretty lass like ye comin' round to visit. Come for the trade, did ye?"

"Aye."

"And how is that jabberin' bastard in black ye follow around, eh?" Bishop asks. "Have ye learned him to keep his tongue yet?"

I grin. "I believe Sarah keeps it in a jar."

Bishop's laugh devolves into another coughing fit.

I near wish I had not made the jest, until he gains control of his breath again.

"Tried to warn him, I did," Bishop says. "But it's not many men what can turn from a pretty face. How is yer sister? Didn't happen to bring her, did ye?"

I shake my head.

"Pity," he says. "A right fine sight we'd have made. The pair of us gimpin' round together."

"She at least uses her crutches." My left eyebrow rises. "Where are yours?"

"Threw them in the fire for a bit o' kindlin'," Bishop says. "And I'll do the same to the next pair yer brother whittles for me, so don't ye be tellin' him I need another set."

"Grandfather—"

"Don't ye be grandfatherin' me, lass." He growls. "I'm not so old I can't go with ye to take on the raiders I be hearin' about. In truth, I'd hoped ye'd come to ask me join on a war party, rather than come for the trade alone."

"Would that we could go to war together," I say. "I have oft wished to accompany Father on such a party against our enemies."

"Which enemies would that be?"

My face puzzles at his question. "Do you not mean the Iroquois? George said—"

Bishop snorts me silent and claps his hands together, rubbing them together as he leans forward. "Can it be ye don't know then? Did yer brother not tell ye what news we've had from the east?"

I shake my head and see his face light with devilish charm.

He scoots closer to me, indeed, so near me that I smell the whiskey on his breath. Several times, he glances over his shoulder like one expectant of a rap upon the head for speaking out of turn.

"Ye remember the Mathers, dear?" Bishops whispers. "The bastard father and son that hanged me poor wife for a witch, then set their own upon us."

"Increase Mather and his son, Cotton," I say. "Aye, I remember your stories well, Grandfather."

"Don't ye be callin' me grandfather, lass." His voice rises. "Names cause attachment. And I don't do attachments, I remind ye."

"Fine," I say. "But what of the Mathers? We have not spoken of them in years."

"Aye." Bishop's eyes gleam. "But one of them weren't dead then, were they?"

My breath catches in my throat, a sound Bishop chuckles at.

"It be the father dead," he says. "Nigh on four year ago now, though word just came to us of it. Who'd have thought I'd outlive the intolerable Increase Mather, eh?"

He laughs himself into another coughing fit, one that near makes me run to fetch Hannah. He regains control of his infirmity and waves me sit down again.

"But how did you hear tell of this?" I ask. "Surely no brave or French trader brought such news."

Bishop shakes his head. "It were Andrew that heard of it when delivering furs into Sudbury. Met his future bride there too."

I blink my surprise. "A bride?"

"Aye. He means to fetch her come the spring. In truth, yer brother and I are glad of it. Lives with his nightmares, that one. Aye, and tries to drown them in whiskey." Bishop strokes his beard. "For a time, we thought to find Andrew drowned in the river, or else dead in the wild. He yet drinks more than most, but less of late."

"A woman's touch," I say, grateful Andrew has found love at long last.

"Aye," says Bishop. "If only the same could be said of Priest, eh?"

I do not deny his claim. Not only would Bishop know it a lie, but it be one that would taste sour on my tongue.

"Tried to warn them both, I did." Bishop sighs. "He is a wild thing. A wolf with no pack."

"He has a pack," I say quickly.

Bishop grins. "Aye. But ye don't think to tame him like yer sister. Only run free at his side, ye mad she-wolf."

He chuckles anew then fights off another fit.

"I'd run with ye both, if I could, lass. Me spirit's willin', though me bones say no. But if I could..." His voice quiets, his gaze drifting toward the fire. "If I could, I'd see me one last battle ere the banshee shrieks me name and sings me the final song."

I place my hand upon his arm. "I shall take comfort that it be awhile before she comes for you."

Bishop grunts. "Who can say when she comes for us all? As for me, I think me time comes soon." He pats my hand. "Less'n ye find one of the wee bastards to wish her away that is."

I laugh at that. Then settle in beside him, the pair of us relating old memories and happy times. His tiring sooner than I hope saddens me, and so we sit in silence a long while, listening to the logs crackle.

Several times I look sideways at him and think time a cruel trickster, all while giving thanks it lends me more to spend with him. Tears sting my eyes at the thought of how many nights I sat upon Bishop's lap, listening to tales of his homeland and the mysterious creatures residing there.

But today it is his mention of the Mathers that stirs my mind, willing me recall the life before.

I fight such memories off, reminding myself to focus on my time with Bishop while I can. When his head nods, I rise and gather up the bearskin hide upon his bed. I place it over him. Then I stroke his hair back, kiss his brow, and take my leave.

The sun warms my face as I step off the porch.

Across the yard, George has opened the cabin holding his goods. He and some braves stand inside, exchanging pelts for rifles, clothes, and pot ware. Others gather beside a wagon laden with similar goods, trading with a burly stranger.

The bearskin coat the stranger wears fits him well. Some

might mistake such girth for laziness and think him slow. His easy squat to survey the pelts our braves lay at his feet tells me otherwise.

My grin fades when he looks up, his deep-set eyes squinting in study of me, even as he ambles over.

I meet his stare, thinking on Father's teachings that I must never look away.

"You are a fierce one," the trader says to me in the French tongue. "Unlike my wife."

"Where is your wife?"

"She keeps to the kitchen, like a proper wife should." He smiles at me, his teeth black and rotted. He motions to his wagon. "Won't you come see what goods I bring to trade?"

"I need no goods," I say.

"Ah, but every young lady requires something. A pretty dress, perhaps, or a bit of ribbon for your hair. Come." He moves to place his arm around me. "Let me show you—"

I pull my long knife from its sheath, stick the blade to his groin, and feel him hesitate.

"I have no need of your goods, Frenchman." I say to him. "Nor will you find me meek like your wife."

"Aye," he says, wincing. "You are a savage squaw."

"No. My father taught me the ways of the shadow. And like a shadow, you may never touch me." I lean closer to him, whisper. "Test me again and I take what little stones your mother gave you."

He groans when I pull the dagger away, falling to his knees, clutching the small wound I left him.

Braves crow at the sight of the French trader upon my stepping away. Kneeling, I wipe the point of my blade on the grass to clean it, then sheathe the dagger again in my belt and start toward George and Hannah's cabin.

A woman stands upon their porch. Near thick-bodied as the Frenchman, I put her age near fifty and five by the grey in her elsewise russet hair. Her cheeks hang heavy off her jowls, and she frowns at me. Then she disappears inside the cabin, leaving me wonder if I must make ready for a different bout.

-two-

I ENTER MY BROTHER'S HOME AND BASK IN THE COOKING SMELLS— pies resting on the open windowsill to cool, baked cornbread, and venison stew bubbling inside a black kettle.

Hannah does not hear me come in; she busies herself about the hearth.

The large woman I saw outside notices though. She glances up and away as soon as our eyes meet, resuming her task of shucking corn.

"Rebecca," Hannah says. "I have a task for you."

She carries a slew of dead coneys to the opposite end of the table.

She sets them before me. "Would you mind skinning these? You have ever been more skilled at it."

"I shall need a bucket," I say. "My brother should have gutted these in the field for you."

"Aye, and I should have had my husband's hide if it were him who brought them." says Hannah, fetching the bucket. "But they be Andrew's kills."

I snort at that, but keep my quiet at how easily Andrew might have cleaned the lot of these had he stopped to think for a moment. Instead, my gaze strays toward the stranger.

Hannah takes note of my cue. "Ah, how rude of me," she says. "Rebecca, this is my dear friend, Mary Desmaris."

Mary nods in simple acknowledgement, but will not meet my eye.

I know not what to say to one who acts so queer, and I stumble for conversation with her.

"Mary is often shy when meeting new folk," Hannah says. "But you will be hard pressed to find another who works as hard as she. Is that not right, Mary?"

"Aye." Mary mutters.

I pluck my dagger free, and sit to the table. Laying the first coney on its back, I spread its hind legs and dig the tip of my dagger into its soft belly with careful regard not to slice the intestines. I run the blade up the animal's chest and neck, gutting its insides and allowing them fall in the bucket at my feet where they land with a loud *splat.*

"You are good with a knife," says Mary quietly. "Practiced."

"Aye," I reply. "My father saw to that."

"A wise man, no doubt," she says.

I only nod in reply and then loosen the coney's skin from its bones.

"Priest is indeed a goodly soul." Hannah fills the silence betwixt Mary and I. "Whatever your brother may say, I think it good you look to Priest as a father."

"An adopted father, eh?" Mary asks.

I look on Mary as I tear the pelt free from the coney and toss it aside for George to keep if he should wish.

"Well, adopted or no," says Mary, resuming her task. "It be no small blessing to have such a good man around at all, I shouldn't wonder."

"Aye," I say. "I am among the fortunate. He has learned me many things."

"My own father taught me but one. Before his death, that is."

Hannah beams. "Hard work, I should say."

"Obedience." Mary twists an ear of corn. She looks on the skinned coney then offers me a small smile. "It be a goodly thing, your father teaching you the ways of a blade. Better still he taught you how to handle men who would show disrespect."

I follow her gaze out the window.

The French trader yet clutches his groin as he leans upon his wagon. The sound of corn ears, cracking and twisted off, calls my attention. Grimness besets Mary's face as she carries out her task.

"He is your husband then?" I ask.

"Aye," she says. "And I am fortunate to have him."

Her tone makes me dubious of her words, yet I keep my quiet, not wishing intrusion upon her privacy. I instead turn my attention back to my task.

"It is a rare sight to see a girl such as you living among the natives," says Mary. "How came you to be among them?"

Hannah looks on me, and I wonder if she fears I might shrink from such a question.

"Forgive me," says Mary at my lingering silence. "My mind has ever been a curious one and often times when it should not be."

"There is naught to forgive," I say. "I have no fear of words."

Hannah smiles at me. "Your brother often says the same. A family motto, I think it."

"Perhaps." I turn my attention back to Mary. "I remember little from our life before. Most of my memories hail from the wilderness. The father my brother and sister speak of would never let me venture into the woods alone. He feared natives would take me, I shouldn't wonder."

Mary snorts and points at my attire. "Little good that did."

Her words coax a smile from me. "Aye."

"I heard different," says Hannah. "George says you were ever a mischievous and willful girl. No doubt your father forbidding it enticed you."

I shake my head. "I only recall the freedom I was given after he was taken from this world. My spirit blossomed the moment I stepped into the woods. Time has only deepened my roots."

"And the natives," says Mary. "They accepted you among them with little qualm?"

I bristle at her tone. "Why should they not?" I ask. "We showed them no anger and gratefully accepted the aid they offered."

Mary shrugs. "I have heard many a story of their savagery. Scalping and cannibalism and such tales as are best left unsaid."

I set my knife upon the table and study her face. "You are a Christian, no?"

"Rebecca," says Hannah.

My sister-in-law speaks my name carefully, her voice pleading in hopes I will give up my claim. I ignore it. "Are you a Christian, Mary?"

"Aye," she says.

"Does your god not ask you take eat of his body and drink of his blood in remembrance of him?"

Mary gives me no response, her chin dipping toward her chest, her gaze unable to meet mine.

"Perhaps you should not so quickly judge what you have heard of my people," I say. "And know this also—the natives did not bring scalping into these lands. That were a custom brought over from across the sea. My people honor all living things... even our enemies."

I pick up my knife and stick its blade into another coney. "Should I tell you what works I have seen from white men?"

"No," says Mary quietly. "Of those I have witnessed enough with my own eyes."

I look away from her and see Hannah's disappointment plain. I remind myself I am a guest in her home. Quelling the anger pulsing in me at Mary's claims, I finish the bundle of coneys in little time.

I take up the bucket of entrails, and carry it outside to feed the dogs.

They find me quickly, the lot of them wiggling their tails, begging me give over the meal.

I make them follow me to the barn, their yips entertaining me as I toss the remains into the grass. As the dogs feast, my attention turns to overhearing conversation from the men, the wind breezing through my hair, and the cooking smells wafting across the yard. I delight in all of them.

A whinny from the stables calls me over.

I find my father's stallion, red with a blaze of white upon its chest. Though old and half-blind, I think he must feel my presence for he saunters toward the fencepost and again whinnies at me.

I set the bucket down, leaving it for one of the dogs to lick clean. I approach the pen and climb the fencepost.

The stallion snorts at my touch, yet I do not pull away. Father taught me long ago not to show any beast fear. Only respect.

I place my cheek against the stallion then stroke his jaw and clap his broad neck.

"I've missed you sorely, old friend," I say.

"Hello, Rebecca."

Andrew Martin leans against the barn, his hair unwashed and face unshaven. His hollow eyes look on me, and no little urge to reach for my dagger pulses in me as he takes a drought of the small keg in his hand. He wipes the wet remains away with his stained sleeve.

"Been a long time," he says. "It seems you were a little girl last time I saw you here."

I loathe the way Andrew looks at me, his eyes wandering from my face to my chest.

"But you're not anymore," he says. "Are you?"

My palm rests on the hilt of my dagger. "No, I'm not."

"You yet enjoy playing with knives, I see." He takes another swig of his keg. "I suspect Jacque Desmaris counted himself lucky for your arrival today, that is before you near castrated him. He and his cow wife planned to set out on the morrow. Mayhap they'll leave tonight now that you prowl the trade post."

My fingers quiver at the slight Andrew gives the Frenchman's wife. I quell them by turning the conversation. "I hear you plan to take a wife."

"I do." He kicks at the dirt. "After all, I could not wait a lifetime for you to change your decision."

"And I did not expect you to."

His face darkens at my words, yet I do not take them back.

"My good wishes to you and your bride to come," I say. "May I ask her name?"

"Susannah Barron."

"A goodly name," I say.

"Aye," says Andrew. "And one her father does not wish her to give up. He claims he would not have Susannah live in the wilderness, but I know the truth of it. He does not desire a poor drunkard for a son-in-law."

Andrew chuckles at that, a sound I like not at all.

"I cannot blame him there. Indeed, it seems no one wishes to have me, Rebecca," he says. "None but your brother. And he keeps me out of pity alone."

"My brother does not—"

"He does." Andrew insists. "And for the love I bear him and your family, I cannot make an end of my suffering. I know not how you and George put aside such memories of that night so long ago, but I would be rid of them for good and always if I were able."

He drinks again of the keg, sniffling as he wipes the dregs from his lips.

"I wished you for a wife once. Thought your goodly spirit might rub onto me also." He shakes his head. "I understand now that a whole heart cannot mend a broken one."

"Andrew—"

"Susannah taught me that," he says. "Told me, together, the halves she and I hold between us will make one whole at least." He pauses, struggles to meet my eye. "Forgive my earlier rudeness, I beg you. I had not thought on what to say when first I saw you land upon the shore."

"There is naught to forgive, Andrew," I say. "I am happy for you and will gladly tell your bride the same when meeting her."

"No." His voice shakes. "I would not have you meet her."

I step back. "Why?"

"Susannah has taught me much, and I am glad to take her for my wife," he says. "But it will forever be you to hold my heart, Rebecca. Ruined and broken though it may be, it is yours. For now and always."

I know not what to say to his confession, even as he looks on me for a response.

"You have learned much from Priest," says Andrew. "His quiet way ever did unsettle me. Perhaps I should count myself more fortunate for Susannah's father. For all the verbal threats he gives, his words do not fright me half as much as your adopted father's silence."

Andrew's words coax laughter from me, and he grins.

"Do not think long on my drunken ramblings. I find whiskey the only way to loose my tongue around you." Andrew licks his lips and hesitates to speak. "But I would not have you think poorly of me for it."

"I will not," I say.

Andrew points at the trading cabin and George waving at him. "It seems your brother has need of me after all. Will you come with me, Rebecca, and share the day? No doubt your cunning mind will find ways for all to profit."

"Aye. I should be glad to."

My people and George welcome us among them as we continue the day in trade.

Ciquenackqua alone seems unpleased at the sight of me, and more so when he gives over the pelts owed me for defeating him in our race. "I would win these back from you," he says.

"Why should I risk losing what I've already earned?" I ask. "And especially when you have no more pelts should I win."

He frowns. "Should the ancestors favor you, I will find something of value in trade."

"Very well," I say. "What game should we play?"

"No game," he says. "A wager only. I tire of the claims your aim is equal to Black Pilgrim's."

Deep River steps to my side. "They are no claims, young one. I have seen her aim proven."

"Then let her do so in front of all here today, rather than it be said she took such prey, alone in the woods, with a single shot," says Ciquenackqua. "My father often says we men are liken to beasts of the forest, fleet of foot and clever also, but only a true hunter may take down a bird in flight."

He raises his hand, showing me a wooden orb used for our stickball games.

"I will fling the ball, and I offer you a single shot to put your arrow through it," he says. "I wager the ball falls back to earth untouched."

I nod, and cheers rise from the men as they back away to grant us space.

Ciquenackqua looks on me oddly. "Why do you not nock your arrow?"

"Fling the ball," I say, my tone steady and even.

Ciquenackqua grins then heaves the ball high in the air.

The ball soars above us, my eyes never leaving it. The holes we carved into the sides make it sing, and I tune my ears to its song when the sun's rays blind me. When it falls at the last, I run to catch it.

The men laugh as I turn around and show Ciquenackqua that I hold the ball in hand.

He looks as one confused as his father sighs. "Why do they laugh? She lost the wager."

"No," says Whistling Hare. "She did not."

"But—"

"You wagered the ball would fall to earth untouched, my son. It never reached the ground." Whistling Hare nods at me. "Black Pilgrim taught you well, white squaw."

"She is no squaw," says Deep River. "She has a warrior's spirit. As great as any of us here."

I fight my cheeks from reddening as others whoop in agreement.

Even Whistling Hare grins at that. "Come, my son." He touches Ciquenackqua's shoulder. "Before you think to wager the shirt off your back."

The men laugh.

I do not, seeing Ciquenackqua flush with anger as both he and his father leave our company.

"Ciquenackqua," I call.

When he turns around to see me, I fling the ball skyward. Drawing my long dagger, I tune my ears to the ball's song and wait for it to descend. Then I fling my weapon. The wood cracks as my blade splits through the middle, pinning the remainder against a cabin log.

Ciquenackqua's eyes round and he looks on me in disbelief.

I point at the ball and dagger. "Lest you think I cheated you with clever tricks."

He shakes his head as his father leads him away, all to the tune of more cheers and playful banter as the men congratulate me.

More clans arrive by midafternoon, and soon we are all conversing and trading with one another. Not for the first time, I marvel at how well my brother prospers among the natives. It saddens me to think of those like Mary who will never embrace their goodly nature as George has done.

"You have been asked on," Deep River says to me, late in the afternoon.

"How so?" I ask.

"Braves from a few of the other clans," he says. "Looking for a wife."

I shake my head at such talk. "What did you tell them?"

"I showed them what would happen to any man thinking of you as a simple squaw." He points to the cleaved ball from Ciquenackqua's wager.

"Thank you," I say, laughing with him, "for warding off my suitors."

"Do not tell my wife," he says. "I believe Numees would have you settled and with child that you and she might raise them together."

"She looks to the wrong sister," I say.

"I tell her the same," says Deep River. He points again at my dagger and the ball. "Why did you do that when you had already won the wager?"

My jaw works back and forth as I think on my words. "You and many others in our tribe welcomed my family as your own," I say finally. "But Father teaches me not all in the other clans think the same. He says we must always prove ourselves worthy of being called Miamiak."

"You *are* Miamiak." Deep River clasps my forearm. "And I will have more than words with anyone here who disagrees."

I grip his forearm in return, smiling back even as he yanks to me my feet and bids me join in a game of stickball with he and the other men.

Come the feasting at nightfall, I sit next to George and Hannah. I talk little, preferring to listen to the men boast of hunting stories and other tall tales. The scent of tobacco smoke from the *calumet* they pass round the circle clouds my nostrils. I inhale deep of it, its smell comforting.

Our laughter stops when Whistling Hare and Ciquenackqua approach our fire.

"My father reminds me I gave you no further winnings." Ciquenackqua jerks his necklace free and tosses it at my feet. "This is yours now."

I lift his necklace from the dirt in acceptance of the offering.

He nods in return, fire in his eyes, as they join our circle.

The necklace holds my attention. I rub its stones between my fingers and find one side rough, the other smooth. Experience tells me they are not true stones at all, and I ponder on its familiarity. I don the necklace, though the realization of where I have felt such an oddity before eludes me.

"They are turtle shells," says Ciquenackqua. "My father carved and gifted them to me on the same day he named me."

I look up at my rival of many years and shake my head. "I cannot accept this then."

"You will," says Whistling Hare. "To teach my son wisdom."

Knowing my place, I keep my silence, though I would have Ciquenackqua take the necklace back. I gaze across the fire to our wizened shaman, Creek Jumper, for guidance.

The tattoos round his eyes and cheeks give the impression of an imposing warrior. I have only ever known him gentle, and remember he would call magic from the bones around his neck to chase evil spirits from my dreams.

As with all things, Creek Jumper senses my unease with accepting the necklace.

"It is right Black Pilgrim's daughter keeps this gift," he says.

"Let Ciquenackqua learn from his *manitous* in this matter. That he should be slow to speak and act."

Hannah leans to me, whispers. "I know not this word. What is a *manitous*?"

"The guardian spirit that guides our paths," I say. "Each of us is given one to find and follow if we will seek it out."

The men grow quiet as Creek Jumper takes the *calumet*.

He puffs it several times, blows circles, then passes it on. "My own son will not recall the day he earned his name. His mother and I could not make child for many years and so I prayed to the ancestors. Grant us a child, and I will give what you ask in return."

Creek Jumper places his hand on Deep River's shoulder.

"My son came into this world not long after." Creek Jumper's face turns sullen. "And so I fasted to learn what the ancestors would have of me. In a vision, the water panther, Linnipinja, came to me. Linnipinja say, 'You will give me your son.' Then he showed me where the river moves quick and white from his thrashing tail. 'Bring your son here and honor your promise.'"

A shudder runs through me. I think on the rapids Creek Jumper speaks of and the first time Father took me through them that I might learn fear and respect for Linnipinja's power. I recall also Father's smile as I did not wilt, helping him guide our canoe through the fast water and then safely to shore.

Creek Jumper clears his throat. "My own father had warned many times the water panther drowns men as he wishes, and so I feared giving my son to Linnipinja." Our shaman sighs. "I took him anyway."

My brother and his wife alone seem uncertain of the story. Some of the braves from the other clans lean forward, as I do, the lot of us eager to learn how our friend earned his name.

"Together we went to the white waters. I placed my son in the cradle his mother makes, then gave him to the river." Creek Jumper sits taller. His shoulders back, chest out. "My son did not cry, even as Linnipinja took him under the crashing waves."

Hannah gasps.

My grin broadens to match Creek Jumper's.

"Then I see Linnipinja gives my son back to me. He sweeps him to shore with his guiding tail, my son still in his cradle. Linnipinja say to me, 'You will name your son Deep River, for I took him into my lair and found him strong.'"

Our shaman looks at each of us in turn. We meet his stare with silence, waiting for the lesson he would teach. Creek Jumper's gaze settles on me.

"Tomorrow, Black Pilgrim's adopted daughter starts a path to learn her *manitous*." He grins at me. "Let you think on my story as you fast. Where the *manitous* leads, there you must go. Even if into the water panther's lair."

I breathe deep at his words, my body tingling with the thought of what form my own *manitous* will take. I have long waited this quest and planned the start of my fast accordingly, at a suggestion from Deep River. He warned that fasting in the woods alone took longer to bring on the vision. Instead, I begin mine with the journey home, a reflective trek through the wilderness alongside my friends and adopted family, all of it a reminder of the new life granted me and the promise of what lies ahead.

The night ends too soon for my liking. I bid my brother and his wife goodnight as they retire into their home. Like Father, I prefer sleeping outdoors under the stars and moon.

I retire into my sleeping furs and rub the turtle beads between my fingers as weariness and warmth ushers sleep to take me. All the while, I think on Creek Jumper's words, wondering what path my *manitous* will lead me on and the name awaiting me at its end.

-three-

THE MORNING SUN WAKENS ME, BIDS ME RISE AND PREPARE FOR our leave.

My stomach grumbles in desire as I sit with George and Hannah and watch them break their fast.

I do not partake. Instead, I stave off my hunger with the knowledge my *manitous* will not reveal itself without sacrifice. Still, the smells of Hannah's cooking prove too great a temptation, and I take my leave to find Andrew and bid farewell. I find him nowhere on the ground, and take it as a sign he has spoken his piece to me.

The old bear comes last to see me off, his approach stilted, though he walks without the use of cane or crutch.

"Farewell, lass." Bishop pecks my cheeks, his fuzzy beard tickling me. "Give your sister me love and tell the bastard I said hello."

"I will." I hug him close and drink deep of his familiar smell.

I take my leave of him and join my people by the Wah-Bah-Shik-Ka. We load our goods and hoist the canoes upon our shoulders to bear them over land. I am forced to share the load with Ciquenackqua, he and I being the only two of similar size among the men.

The French trader bears me no love as I wave farewell to his wife, the pair of them readying their own wagon.

My fasting makes the overland return journey to our village harder than I first imagined, but the songs we sing keep my spirit fresh. So, too, do the laughter and stories we share each night beside the fire.

My legs stumble by the time we reach our village, near evening of the fifth day. Weakened by hunger, black spots cloud my vision. Still, the sight of our people gathered in welcome outside the wooden palisades that ring our village lends me strength.

My sister, Sarah, stands out amidst the people, not only for her paler skin or her eternal grimace, but for the dress she wears—blue as the spring sky, sewn of white man's cloth and laced with silk.

I recall the day Father traded beaver pelts, stacked high as a Frenchman's long rifle, for a bolt of cloth to please her. I sigh at the recollection and the knowledge it did not sate her desire for the life before.

She hobbles toward me, leaning heavy on the crutches Father fashioned her.

My gaze homes on the furred pads beneath her arms, notes the padding is worn from heavy use. I remind myself to hunt a few squirrels after my fast and use their hides to replenish her comfort.

"Good morrow, sister," says Sarah. "I have missed you sorely."

"Aye, and I you. The others send their love and wish you would visit at the next trading."

Sarah frowns. "Come. I would hear all about our brother and Bishop." Her eyes meander to my neck. "And how you came by such a pretty necklace."

I laugh that she should notice, though she were ever observant of such things.

We take our time entering the village, pausing whenever she needs to give her legs rest.

It pains me that Sarah's body works against her, though I hide my feelings and continue telling her of our time at the trade post. We work our way through the maze of *wikiamis*, dome-shaped huts crafted of saplings tied together and covered with bark and animal skins.

We reach our own, and I pull back the buckskin flap to allow Sarah enter first.

The scent of smoke and spices hangs heavy in our hut.

I sit cross-legged beside the fire, listening to it sing with crackling *pops*. Its light casts long shadows of my sister and me against the far wall. They dance in time with the flickering flames.

A black bear's stretched hide lies before me. I glide my fingers through its soft fur, parting hairs in my wake. Even now, I find it easy recalling the day I tracked the beast to its lair. Easier still remembering the faces of those who mocked me.

None are so foolish now.

Indeed, few braves can match my aim with bow or rifle. Only one can best me with the tomahawk and the long knife.

Only Father.

New pelts lay upon the floor, and I study the hides—elk, beaver, fox. My thoughts turn to memories of tracking such worthy creatures with Father. I honor them again with silent thanks for the lessons each taught me during the many hunts. Yet for all the pelts before me, I know the bounty lacks one prized hide—the elusive trickster of the forest. The only pelt I have yet to acquire.

Seated across the fire, I catch Sarah watching me.

I am no stranger to the look she gives. Many of the squaws in our village disapprove that I should go into the wood alongside our braves to fetch game and pelts for the trading posts.

But my sister is no squaw, and the disapproval in her eyes cuts worse.

"You should not look on the furs in such a way, Rebecca," Sarah says. "You have only just returned from our brother's post. Can we not sit and talk together without your attention turning to hunting and hides?"

My fingers dig deeper, clutching tufts of fur. "Father would not care."

Sarah shakes her head. "I have asked you more than once to cease such pretenses."

She wraps a bit of tanned leather round a bundle of pelts. Jerk the knot tight.

"Our father died long ago. My husband remains—" She levels me with her eyes. "And Priest will never be father to you. No matter how you might wish it."

I know that I should hold my silence in keeping with Father's lessons. My sister does not often fall into such a foul spirit, but I have learned to tread lightly when such a mood strikes her.

Still, for all Father's teachings, I have not yet mastered his skillful, quiet way.

"Your husband *is* Father to me," I say. "More so than the other one you speak of. That man is but a shadow in my memory."

Sarah grimaces. "Odd that you should say so. I recall our true father showed you more favor than ever he did for George or me."

She ties the other end of the pelt bundle, and chuckles in a way I like not at all.

"Perhaps it is just," says Sarah. "That you also think of Priest in such a goodly manner. You were ever the only one to coax the smallest of smiles from our real father. Why should you not also steal my husband's affections?"

Her biting words swell anger within me. Still, my conscience warns I am partially to blame for goading her. I humble myself, as Sarah oft preaches her god would have us do, and steady my tone. "Sister—"

"Do you think I cannot not see him turn from me?" Sarah asks. "I may be crippled, but I am not blind."

"You wrong me," I say, noticing her cheeks glisten in the firelight. "And him also to speak so."

My sister shakes her head and busies herself with tying another leather strip 'round the bundle of pelts in her lap. Her fingers work deftly, far more skillful than mine at such tasks.

"My husband is a good man, and true, but even the best of men crave youth and beauty. And I—" Sarah's voice flutters. "I grow older, Becca. My womb barren, no matter the prayers I offer God to heal me."

She sets the finished bundle aside and folds her hands in her lap while I struggle to think of what words to say.

"I-I give my husband no sons," she says. "Not even a daughter with a wild spirit to match his own. Why should he not turn from me when one such as you shares our hut?"

"Sarah—"

"You have ever been the more beautiful sister." Sarah looks at me, tears spilling down her cheeks. "Must you be the wilder also?"

I rise, thinking I might go to her and offer some little comfort.

The earth spins beneath me.

My head swoons from the hunger pains I have endured the past week in preparation for the dream fast. My stomach grumbles in warning that my vision comes soon.

The moment passes, and I abandon my own bundle to cross the distance between us. I hold Sarah in my arms, embracing my sister with a tenderness not shown between the pair of us in many a year.

Her body shakes, trembles as she clutches me closer.

"I have naught, Becca...naught to offer my husband but grief," Sarah says, her voice a whimper. "A darkness lives within me ever since the night I slew Hecate, I swear it on my soul. Th-The Devil's daughter laid a curse upon me that God will not lift."

I know not how to ease my sister's mind, for the god she speaks of is but another foreign memory to me. A relic from the life before, like the father she recalls and I do not. Indeed, as a river divides one bank from the other, Sarah's mention of her god reminds me time serves only to further the distance betwixt us.

No small part of me wonders if the rift will ever be healed.

"The white man's devil has no power here." I stroke Sarah's hair. "Creek Jumper would fend away such an evil spirit with his magic. Just as he warded off the sickness in your legs once."

I regret my words the moment I speak them.

My sister collapses into another fit of tears. "Your shaman has no power, Becca."

"He does," I say. "I have seen it. With you and—"

"Then why can I not stand of my own power?" Sarah asks. "What cruel sorcery is this that I may walk one day and not the next? No...no man, or shaman, can heal me. This curse is the Devil's work, sister. Only God can heal me."

I keep my silence this time, though knowing well the reason Creek Jumper's medicine does not keep. The old ones say my sister has not renounced the white man's ways. They believe Sarah, like Bishop and George, will always cling to the life our family led in the time before.

Not like me.

Not like Father.

"But I fear, sister," says Sarah. "I fear He brought this torment upon me for my sins. M-my legs grow weaker each passing season. I think it be God's intent for me to slither on my belly the rest of my days…my punishment for murdering Hecate."

"No." I pull away, staring into Sarah's tear-stained eyes that she might understand I speak true. "You saved many that night, and if your god would punish such an act, mayhap you follow the wrong spirit."

I point to my sister's bed of furs, toward her Bible and the bundle she keeps hidden away—the journal of Thomas Putnam, given her by Hecate. The same book Father insisted I read over and again until I could recite the names and histories of all who would mean us harm.

"If you believe Putnam's words, you know the evil done Abigail Williams in her youth tortured her the rest of her days and drove her to become Hecate. Fath—" I stop myself for fear of angering Sarah further. "*Priest* often reminds me to give thanks after making a kill in the wood, do the creature honor as they make their journey on the spirit path."

"You speak of slaying beasts, Rebecca," says Sarah. "You have never murdered."

"I would, if need be." I release my hold on her and rise to leave. Dizzied by the hunger pain, I struggle to keep my balance as I stand. "Man or beast, all have a spirit, sister. You believe you killed Hecate. I say you freed the spirit of Abigail Williams."

Sarah does not reach for me again. She looks up from the fire, her face pale and tired. "And who will free me of my pain, sweet sister? You?"

I sneer. "Priest would rage to hear you speak such nonsense."

"His anger would please me greatly." Sarah scoffs. "A welcome change from the damnable silence he shields himself with."

"You loved that about him once," I chide her.

She smiles at that—a sight to warm my soul.

It vanishes too soon.

"Did you know Mother once told me our father changed his evil ways after taking her to wife?" Sarah asks.

"Aye," I say. "You have mentioned it."

Sarah nods. "Mother said he put aside his Salem sins and became a godly man. The man we knew as Paul Kelly."

Sarah fiddles with a bit of leather, and I wonder what catches on her tongue that she cannot speak on it.

"Mother said she had nothing to offer him but forgiveness and that he took on gladly. Such a noble act from them both, no?" Sarah looks on me as if for approval. "For he to change and her to forgive..."

I ache for her hurting, though wishing to understand her meaning better. I keep my silence, watching Sarah wipe the corners of her eyes.

"I have offered my own husband forgiveness and more." Her chin dips. "Yet he will not accept it."

"Perhaps he cannot." I venture. "Or mayhap he feels no regret for the things he has done."

I do not tell my sister that I only argue thusly because I have no regrets. Still, I wonder what Father did to make my sister speak plain with such offerings of forgiveness.

She does not answer my argument quickly. Her gaze returns to the fire, eyes widening at its brightness.

"He does," she says. "My husband regrets, though he will not speak if I be one of them."

I step closer. "How can you claim such things, sister? No one can know the inner thoughts of another."

"He spoke them one night." Sarah's voice deepens. "He and George, aye, and Andrew Martin also. They had all drunk so deep of the firewater to make my husband sleep, though his restlessness kept me awake. He cried out, aye, howl be a better term for it, in such a manner to haunt my dreams from that night to this. And at the last, still deep in his torment, Priest uttered but a single word...*mercy*."

A shiver runs down my spine. "What pain could have caused him to cry out thusly?"

"I know not," says Sarah. "He would not say the following morn, or any morn after. I half believe he hoped I would forget the matter."

Though I make no claim against her, I know in my soul Father would never expect such a thing. My sister forgets nothing.

"Can you believe I thought to learn his secrets when first he and I met so long ago?" Sarah asks, shaking her head. "But he and his silence are one. Nothing penetrates it. Not even a wife's love."

"If Priest were not content with you, he would leave," I say.

"And so he does," says Sarah, her eyebrows raised. "Into the woods with you, or else warring on other tribes. The Black Pilgrim has no time for a wife."

"Do not twist my words." I fight to keep the anger inside me. "You knew my meaning. Either of you may leave the other if and when you see fit. No law binds you and he together."

"Duty binds him to me," Sarah says. "Nothing more."

"Then think what ill you will of him," I say, standing. "I know otherwise."

"You claim to know my husband better than I?" Sarah asks.

"In this matter, aye."

Tired of her discontent, I step to leave our home.

"Mayhap you are right," Sarah whispers. "After all, you and he have spent many a night in the wood together while at the hunt. He has ever been a shadow in my home."

A sister's bond calls me back. Sarah sits forlorn beside the fire and the bundles of fur. The sheer number of them speaks plain to the time he and I have spent tracking together. All of it time she could not spend with us.

"And like a shadow, Priest will never abandon you," I say. "Nor will I."

Sarah frowns. "You already have, sis—"

An ominous sound outside our hut cuts my sister short. The rhythm comes slow and steady, approaching from the northeast.

My sister's face pales. "Drums..." she says, her breath rapid.

My body turns cold at her nervousness, she having been sore affrighted of beating drums since ever I can remember. I have no such fear, and reach for the weapons tucked in my belt. I loose both my tomahawk and long knife, and bring them to bear, even as I struggle to control my wits.

"Drums, Rebecca..." Sarah says. "Were there a dance planned for this evening?"

I raise my hand, ushering her silent.

My ears well recognize the music drawing steadily toward our village, even if my sister's do not.

The approaching drums play not for the corn dance, or even feasting.

The drums call for war.

-four-

I BURST OUT OF OUR HUT AND FIND OUR VILLAGE BUSTLING.

Young braves whoop as they race toward our village's main entry, many of them bearing torches. Children follow their lead with barking dogs running alongside them. The elderly move slower, escorted by squaws. The faces of the old ones tell me there be no enemy among us yet.

My pulse slows, and I pause to listen again on the drums.

They sound more familiar now—similar to our own, and yet not.

"Becca!"

I turn to find my friend and heart-sister, Numees, wife of Deep River.

Tall and lithe, I envy her copper skin and natural beauty. Beaded quillwork adorns her buckskin dress, the design marking her as possessing an artful hand. She stands outside the shared hut of her mother-in-law, shouldering a buckskin robe to fight the fall chill.

Not for the first time, I think it little coincidence our homes neighbor one another.

Numees and I share a bond not like many in our village, both of us outsiders when first we came to live here as children. Though I am white and she Mohican, our tribe welcomed us both to dry the tears of those in mourning.

Now we are both Miamiak.

"Becca!" Numees waves again.

I acknowledge her with a wave of my hand. "Where is your husband?"

"Gone to meet the war party with the other men," says Numees. "Does your father not join them?"

"I know not where he is." I look back to my home, thinking of Sarah inside. Again I turn to Numees. "I would know more of who beats these drums. Will you look after my sister?"

She nods. "Go."

I sprint for the main entrance to our village, calling swiftness from my legs. My head pounds from the absence of food. I will myself on, weaving around the other bowl-shaped homes in my path.

A few braves guard the ring of wooden palisades encircling our village. Their presence gives me further peace of mind at leaving my sister with Numees.

I pass the council longhouse, and see familiar faces shouldering logs that require three men to carry. They bear the wood to the sprawling center of our village. The lean-to stack they build has the makings of a great fire to come. My mind wonders for what purpose.

A horde of braves congregates across the open space, their backs to me.

I cross the empty field quick enough, entering the throng. The men relent in my maneuvering for a better view, a sign I have earned my place among them. I halt near the front, just inside the opening to our village.

A lone sentry stands beyond our protective wall—our peace chief, Sturdy Oak. Shirtless, despite the cold, the tattoos of our people adorn his body. His face seems stone carved, giving no sign of his thoughts to the train of torches crawling toward us from the woods.

"Where is our war chief?" A brave whispers behind me. "Why does he not stand with Sturdy Oak? Both should be here."

His question reflects my own, though the beating drums give me little time to dwell on such thoughts. I stand as one with the group, the murmurs growing silent when a lone stranger steps away from the woodland safety and onto our territory.

He walks beside his horses, signaling he comes in peace, and he wears a necklace of bear claws. His scarred body reflects the fierceness radiating in his face.

I am conflicted whether I dislike his prideful air or respect it, even as my gaze lowers to the *wampum* belt he bears toward our chieftain. I stare at the belt, admiring the handsome make of shell beads strung together. Its beads appear crimson in the torchlight, their original hue dyed to match the color of war.

"Greetings to you, cousins," says the brave, his voice deep and gaze penetrating. "I am called Two Ravens. My people and I would ask you join us on the war path."

"And whom do you mean to war upon?" our chief asks.

"The Iroquois," says Two Ravens.

My eyes widen at such a claim, and those behind me gasp.

Two Ravens seems pleased with our reactions, judging the look on his face.

My chief's laughter cuts the tension. "I think you are a madman, or have toked too long of the *calumet*."

The foreign chief grins.

"You sound like my wife, Grandfather," says Two Ravens. "And yet, you speak true of my love for the smoke pipe. But call me no madman."

"What would you have me name one who asks us to war on the Iroquois?"

"Defender of the people," says Two Ravens. "Survivors from a lesser tribe to the northeast came among us seeking refuge with odd claims a rogue band warred on them. Those who escaped said the raiders were Mohawk. Others believe the Seneca."

"How is that odd?" asks Sturdy Oak. "The Iroquois are a united nation. Each aiding the other in battle when agreed upon."

"I speak of a different oddness," says Two Ravens. "The survivors say these warriors fought with uncommon strength. One not gifted ordinary men."

Whispers ensue among my people, fear of an unseen threat. It would catch me also if I lent the words such credence. A memory from the life before stirs within me. I fight it off, not wishing to give sway to such thoughts when I should face the here and now.

"The survivors said also that women fought alongside the braves."

"Squaws?" our chief says.

"I said nothing of squaws," says Two Ravens, finding my face in the crowd. "They say those who fought were white women."

He points at me. "You, girl. Come. I would look upon your pale face, much as I despise it."

My fingers clench the handles of my weapons as I step forward, rather than be thought a coward. I meet his gaze and keep his stare, never glancing away, even as his eyes work over me.

Two Ravens laughs. "Why, it is no pale face that stands before me. It is a fearsome squaw."

I glare at Two Ravens that he might understand his words truer than he realizes.

"Tell me, girl, how did you come to live among these peace lovers? Desire for war marks your face." Two Ravens studies me closer still. "Would you avenge our fallen cousins? Or do you live here for another purpose?"

I do not take his meaning. My face must reveal such for our chief comes to my aid.

"She is no traitor," says Sturdy Oak. "The girl came among us near fifteen year ago. She and her sister."

Two Ravens sneers. "You keep two of these among you then?"

My fingers quiver on the edge of my long knife. I study the neck of Two Ravens, wonder if I could have my knife to it before he might react.

"Two Ravens speaks with hate," says Sturdy Oak, his tone grave as he moves between us. "I see no pale faces here, only some Miamiak lighter-skinned than others. And we protect all that we name family."

Two Ravens snorts. "My men and I came seeking braves. Yet we find only squealing boys and white dogs among you. We heard your tribe led by a proven war chief. A brave who knows neither fear nor defeat."

I open my mouth to speak.

Sturdy Oak places his arm about me. "You heard true, though I know not where my adopted son may be. The woods call his name more than most."

"Can you not send messengers to find him?" Two Ravens asks. "I would speak with him now."

"Send all you wish," says Sturdy Oak. "None will find him unless he would be seen."

"Fool." Two Ravens grabs his necklace. "Do you not see the long claws around my neck? I can find anyone."

"Then let you search for my adopted son," says my chief, his tone steady.

I find myself wishing Two Ravens would hunt for Father, more that I wish my presence there when Father finds him.

"I wait for no man," says Two Ravens. "My braves and I would make the war dance with you this eve and set out tomorrow to avenge our fallen cousins."

"Our men ride nowhere without our war chief's leave," says Sturdy Oak.

Two Ravens swings astride his horse, his lip curling as he holds the war belt in his fist. He lifts it high in the air and parades before the men in our village.

"Who of you will come with us?" He shouts. "Who will reap vengeance upon our enemies?"

His confidence sings to me. It calls me to whoop and follow, despite my misgivings of his character. The thought of making the war dance excites me more even than the thrill of the hunt. I find myself not alone in such thoughts. A single look over my shoulder reveals that Two Ravens holds the younger men in our tribe also in his sway.

"Would you have the Miamiak known as peace lovers," Two Ravens asks our people, "or ride with me and war upon the Iroquois?"

One brave whoops. His reaction sets others to the same.

Sturdy Oak pulls me close, his hand rough, but comforting. His long grey hair brushes my cheeks. It smells of tobacco and smoke, home and safety.

Two Ravens continues his parade. His stallion near kicks me as it rears. He gains control over the beast, then looks upon me. "And you, squaw? Will you come with us?"

He extends the war belt toward me. The shell beads rattle against one another, a miniature set of drums beating the same alluring call. Their red beads promise glory if I will but take the opportunity.

An arrow whistles past my ear, giving me no chance.

Others gasp and my muscles tighten at the sound.

Where once Two Ravens held the war belt, now it has vanished.

My eyes sweep the area and find the arrow's shaft embedded in a wood palisade behind me. The war belt hangs from it, skewered like a squirrel to a tree.

Two Ravens raises his tomahawk. "Who dare—"

A shadow steadily approaches from the tree line, his hardened gaze set on this foreign chief come to our village.

"Who is that brave?" Two Ravens asks.

"My adopted son," says our chief. "And the man you seek."

Two Ravens sneers. "But he is a white man."

Sturdy Oak places his hand upon my wrist, halting me from drawing my long knife at the insult to my father's honor. "Once," he says to Two Ravens. "Now he and his family are of the people."

Father passes Two Ravens without acknowledgement. He continues to the palisade and retrieves his arrow. Looks long on the war belt as if discerning each of its shell beads.

I wonder what he must think of these newcomers and their call for battle. He has never been warm to strangers, and colder still to those who speak more than listen. Still, that my Father continues his study of the war belt says much to me.

"Does your white dog not speak, Grandfather?" Two Ravens asks, sliding off his stallion. "Or would you have me teach him?"

"He speaks little," says Sturdy Oak. "And the wise heed his words."

Two Ravens laughs. "I am no wise man. My people appointed me for my love of battle." He points his tomahawk at my father. "You claim him as your war chief. I will see him fight."

For the first time, my father looks on Two Ravens. Like the eagle, Father's stare does not waver. He sheds his black cloak and stands bare-chested in the firelight. Tattoos grace his body—runes of our people and scriptures from the Bible my sister keeps.

Father hands me the war belt before approaching his opponent.

My fingers roll over the smooth beads, twisting them on their leather strands. Their gentle rattle and my hunger pains call me to enter my dream fast. I fight the feeling away, knowing I must seek solitude for the vision to take full hold over me.

I turn instead to see Father and Two Ravens circling one another.

Two Ravens lunges first.

Father easily steps aside and dodges the immediate backlash Two Ravens makes with his tomahawk.

The blade swings wide.

Father rushes in to take hold of its handle.

Surprise crosses the face of Two Ravens. Then fury.

He catches my father's neck, squeezes.

I dart forward when he gasps.

Sturdy Oak halts me, even as Father twists the wrist of Two Ravens and steals his tomahawk.

Father swings the butt of it up, catching Two Ravens under the chin, knocking him back.

My blood rushes as Father dives at his opponent, spearing him to the ground. He rises atop Two Ravens, and the tomahawk whistles as he spins its handle in his hand until its blade again points to the sky.

Father swings the tomahawk down, burying the blade in earth, an inch from the ear of Two Ravens.

Silence hangs in the air, broken only when Two Ravens laughs.

The sound catches me—aye, and my people—with its good-hearted nature.

My father stands over his opponent.

Though defeated, Two Ravens smiles. "It seems we both spoke true, peace chief." His gaze flits to Sturdy Oak. "You took in a white dog."

He raises his hand to father in request to help him stand.

My father yanks him to his feet.

Two Ravens claps Father on the shoulder. "But he is a wild one."

I find the foreign chief's grin infectious, even while my father keeps his grim façade.

"And a wild dog I would gladly make the war dance with." Two Ravens continues. "If he will treat with me and hear what I would say."

My father joins me, placing his hand upon my arm, his touch warm and comforting.

I look into his eyes and feel my spirits rise with pride. I offer him the war belt with both hands.

He does not take it quickly, only looks on it again with a studiousness I have seen him wear only in the woods. Yet where his eyes appear curious and gay while at study on the hunt, now I think they seem tired, wary of what the beads would call from him and our people.

His gaze finds mine.

A shudder runs through me at the volumes his silence speaks. I wonder how my sister does not understand his quiet way and why she would change him if she held such power.

Father takes the war belt from me.

I know in my soul how he will answer the call of Two Ravens.

Our people go to war on the morrow.

I only hope they think me worthy enough to join them.

-five-

I sit beside Numees, the pair of us mending moccasins and hides. My mind turns to the council longhouse where the men of our tribe, and of Two Ravens', discuss whether or not to make the war dance.

I look to the night sky, finding the moon not yet at its fullest peak.

"The hour draws late," says Numees. "Our men have been at the council fire a long time."

"Too long." I say.

"Should decisions of war be made quickly?" Numees chuckles. "My husband says your father asks each brave to speak his mind in such council matters."

I nod in reply. Remind myself to focus on the task at hand.

"Deep River thinks your father wise in this," says Numees. "As do I."

"And I also," I say, lest she think I do not support Father's decisions.

Numees elbows me playfully. "But you wish he asked your opinion too."

I grin. "I do not care if he should ask my opinion. Only hear my request to follow him on his path."

"You are a strange squaw." Numees laughs.

I thread a bit of leather through a moccasin. "I have heard

other tribes allow their women to make decisions of war and appointing chieftains."

"Decisions only. Their squaws do not make the war dance, as you would." Numees says, not unkindly.

I look deep into my friend's amber eyes. "Have you never felt the dance's call? Does nothing stir when the old ones lay their hands upon the drums?"

"I feel stirrings, aye, as do all in the tribe. But the battle call?" Numees shakes her head. "I know my place in this world. It is at my husband's side."

My face must give my thoughts away.

Numees glances away. "Perhaps you find me odd..."

"I find you happy." I smile. "And think it must be pleasing to know your path."

"It was not always so. When the Mohawk killed my family, my path led to slavery." She hesitates. "Many a night, I dreamt of ending my life that I might walk the spirit trail with my mother and father."

"Why did you not?"

"I tried," she says. "Ran one night, thinking their men would find and kill me for disobeying them. Instead, I lost myself to wandering the forest for many days. A dream fast took me one night, and I saw a cloudy sky break with raindrops upon my forehead. I woke to find a shadow carrying me away from that lost place. The same shadow that brought me here."

My brow wrinkles at her tale.

Numees looks at me, her eyes shining. "Your father."

I put down my moccasin. "Why have you never told me this before?"

"I felt no need," she says. "I tell you only tonight because you seem troubled."

"I am."

"With your sister?" she asks.

"With many things," I reply. "My own path most of all."

Numees finishes her mending and takes up another moccasin. "Creek Jumper says paths are ever-changing. Snaking through woods or rivers, but always leading us."

I dwell on her words a moment and think on their wisdom, especially as her mention hails from our shaman.

"When I was younger," I say, "I tried looking back on what events led me to this place, but in truth, I do not recall most of it. Creek Jumper says I buried memories of the life before to shield my mind."

"You remember nothing?"

"Some things," I say. "Screaming faces...fire...fear...and—"

I look up and see my sister, far across the gathering place.

Sarah limps around the fire, leaning on a wooden crutch fashioned special for her. She wipes her brow and brushes aside strands of dark hair she claims were gifted her by our true father.

I think on how Sarah oft claims I am the prettier sister, yet looking on her now, I know myself the lesser.

"Sacrifice," I tell Numees. "Great sacrifice."

Sarah catches me watching her.

I avert my gaze back to mending the moccasins.

To her credit, Numees asks me to speak no more of my sister, or of the night that caused Sarah's infirmity.

"The *manitous* demand great sacrifices from us all," she says, after a time. "Perhaps yours will learn you what it would have in exchange for its gifts."

While I ponder on her words, Numees hums a Mohican tune I have oft heard her sing while around her home fire.

My thoughts question what form my *manitous* will take. More than anything, I hope it will be a wild spirit—a snarling she-bear, perhaps, or a cunning wolf.

The wafting scents of food distract my hopes and set my stomach to rumbling anew.

I curse the delicious odors and that we must sit so near the cook fires. I had chosen to aid in mending moccasins and hides to avoid such temptation. Instead, I smell Three Sisters stew—corn, beans, and squash—and see the golden hue of cornbread set aside for feasting. Bits of elk roast over the fire, dripping fat licked by the flames.

Tonight, all will feast.

All save me.

My sight meanders to the sweat lodge near the council longhouse. Again, I ponder on what spirit will seek me out to guide me on my path.

The weakness in my flesh warns the answer comes soon.

I drive away the scents of food by pricking my finger. The bone needle I use to thread the moccasins cuts sharp and serves my purpose well. I rub the blood droplets with my fingers and look on its scarlet color in the firelight. The mere sight forces me to swoon and calls my spirit to a different hunger, one not slaked by feasting on Three Sisters stew or even elk meat.

"Becca..." says Numees.

I look away from my finger and follow her point.

Our shaman, Creek Jumper, has left the council longhouse. His gait steady and sure, he looks at no one as he leaves the gathering place, carrying a bundled fox pelt in hand.

I stand with the others in my tribe. We gather around as Two Ravens and his men empty out of the longhouse. Not a one gives any sign as to the council's decision.

Anger swells within me as Ciquenackqua emerges, his head held high. His father, Whistling Hare, follows him out, acknowledging our people with a curt nod.

Sturdy Oak and Father exit last. Like the horned owl whose feathers he wears tied in his hair, Father masks his emotions with fierceness. He strides toward Two Ravens, holding the *calumet* in his left hand.

"My people," says Sturdy Oak, calling my attention. "We have met with our cousin tribe and listened to all they would say. Two Ravens asks us to make war on a mighty people and avenge those we do not know. I counsel we, too, are like to have no people if we fight such a powerful nation."

I expect such from our peace chief, yet having sat with Father at Sturdy Oak's fire many a night, I know him wise where others might deem him cowardly. Our peace chief must believe we cannot win this fight.

"We are a fierce and proud people," Sturdy Oak continues. "But even the strongest bear cannot withstand a pack of wolves. We are one nation. The Iroquois are six united, since the Tuscarora joined them five years past."

Our peace chief raises his arms as if imploring us to heed him.

"Two Ravens says the French will join our cause." Sturdy Oak shakes his head. "I say the English will rally to the Iroquois. All this and more we spoke over the smoke pipe. I would keep our men from this fight, but this is matter of war. Its final decision lies with my son and war chief, Black Pilgrim. He will decide."

Father steps forward, and my eyes flit to Sarah. Her face resigned, as if it matters not what the decision will be.

My heart turns icy at her resignation and that she does not stand supportive as any good wife should do. My stare swivels from her and back to Father.

He stands between Sturdy Oak and Two Ravens, his gaze locked on the *calumet*.

I wonder what answers he believes lay in the pipe for it to hold his attention.

He looks up, and I believe he searches for Sarah, yet he passes over her with little regard. Only when his eyes find mine does he hesitate. His eyes squint, and his face sets in grim determination.

His left hand shoots to the sky, holding the *calumet* high over his head.

Someone in our crowd shouts a war cry. Others take up its echo until I swear even my brother at his trading post will hear.

A broad grin breaks across the face of Two Ravens. He and Father grasp each other's forearms, symbolizing the new union betwixt our tribes.

Drums mix with the jubilant war cries, and I smile at their combined meaning.

Numees takes my hand. She and I join our tribe, gathering round the bonfire. Together we sit among other familiar faces, all of us awaiting the ceremony to come. I search around the circle and see myself not the only one enthralled.

The young ones watch the old in eager wait. Not a few of the elderly keep time with the drums. Some nod their heads. Others pat the backs of their grandchildren's hands, teaching them the beat.

My soul warms at the sight, recalling Sturdy Oak's wife once teaching me to keep rhythm in a likewise manner. The memory changes upon noticing my sister limping away from the circle, back to our home I suppose.

I shake my head at her disapproval. Alter my attention, looking through the flames at Father.

Seated amongst the braves, he does not stand out so easily. The old ones say even the sun recognizes him as Miamiak and that it turned Father's skin copper to better suit his place among the people. Father stares into the blaze, his stoicism unchecked, while the other men congratulate one another.

I, too, look on the fire as if it might reveal to me the answer my father seeks.

But even its flames seem subject to the beating of drums as the old ones sing the ancient song, their withered voices falling in time with the drum cadence.

The power of the collective resonates in my soul.

Like long shadows in the waning hours of day, four figures rise to make their presence known. They dance—bending and bowing, rising and falling—their movements keeping time as one.

My friend and Numees' husband dances closest to us. Firelight sheens off his shaved head as he deftly spins around the circle, marking him an experienced brave who has long practiced the war dance. The first to reach the striking pole, he gashes it with his long dagger.

"I am Deep River," he says, pounding his chest. "And gladly walk the warpath with my brothers. I ask they allow me first into battle. Like the name my father gives me, I will drown the Iroquois in a deep river of blood."

I cheer with Numees and several others as he steps aside for Ciquenackqua's father.

Whistling Hare moves in longer strides, sweeping 'round the fire. He looks a crazed person, to my mind, yet I find myself drawn to his determination for the dance. He strikes the pole hard with a long wooden club, its end fashioned like eagle talons grasping a smooth, stone ball.

"It is only right that *I* draw first blood from the Iroquois," he says. "I do not dance tonight that any brave here might steal my glory. I fight only so more people might witness the greatness of Whistling Hare."

I laugh with the many others in my tribe at such a bold statement.

"This will be my son's first time upon the war path," says Whistling Hare. "Let him dance now. For one day, others will hear his name and tremble."

With his club, Whistling Hare ushers Ciquenackqua follow his example.

Unlike the two before him, I find my rival's dance lacking. His gait stilted and unsure, he attempts to distract our attention by waving his arms over his head.

It serves only to raise my ire further. My mind shouts to stand and show our people that I, too, can make the war dance. Aye, and dance it better than he, for I have oft practiced when alone in the wood.

Instead, I remain seated, forced to watch his lance glance off the pole.

"I-I am Ciquenackqua." His voice breaks.

"Louder, boy." Whistling Hare roars. "I did not grant you such a name that you would hide inside your shell."

Not a few laughs rise from the men Two Ravens brought.

Our people keep silent, showing respect even to one who might not give the same in return.

"I am Ciquenackqua," he says, his voice near shouting. "Like the great snapper, I will tear our enemy to pieces."

Our tribe shouts approval.

Ciquenackqua retires to his father's side, all his former pride restored and then some.

The raucous cheers cease as the final dancer strides round the fire.

His movements more fluid and sure than any before him, Father dances with the quiet grace and stealth of a mountain lion. To judge his expression, I gather he has shut himself from this world, his very soul possessed by the drums.

I have often witnessed him wear a similar look while on the hunt.

The fire and the dance are all that matter to him now, and I hold no pretense he sees me at all as he passes.

Father buries his tomahawk into the war pole, leaving its blade stuck deep for all to see.

I smirk at the stunned faces on the foreign tribe and note the eyes of Two Ravens round as a great owl's.

Unlike the others, Father makes no impassioned speech, nor claim. He only looks around the circle that all might know he will never be first to shy away. When he steps aside, a cry to dwarf those gone before him rises from both tribes.

I add my voice to all the others as a fifth dancer emerges from the crowd—our shaman, Creek Jumper.

I understand now why he left our midst after the council decision—he has painted the whole of his face white with red tears upon his cheeks. He dances faster than the others, chanting. Pulling small bones from the leather pouch worn round his neck.

One by one, Creek Jumper fells each of the former dancers with the power he keeps hidden in the bones. Only when he finishes his victory circle does he bring each dancer back to life with the charms granted him.

I lean forward, anxious to learn what gifts the warriors will offer as Creek Jumper unclasps his buckskin cloak and lays it upon the ground.

He backs away, clutching his leather pouch, muttering prayers as the dancers step forward to present their offerings.

Deep River is first to produce his gift, laying a lock of his wife's hair upon the cloak before rejoining us.

Next, Whistling Hare empties a small bag of tobacco.

For all his early pride, I take note that Ciquenackqua warily approaches the cloak and our shaman's watchful eyes. Dropping to his knee, he places a small turtle shell upon the cloak then hastens to his father.

Again, I find myself envying the boy. Not only is he permitted to make the war dance, he knows the form his *manitous* takes. I will the weakness in my flesh to quicken the dream fast that I too might recognize my guardian spirit and provide a worthy gift.

For all my desire, I am forced to wait and watch.

Father steps last to the cloak, his hands cupped around his contribution. His fingers open slowly, sifting a dusky snow between them to cloud over the other offerings.

Creek Jumper nods as Father rejoins the circle. "Tonight we welcome Two Ravens and our new brothers in war. We thank our *manitous* and ask that they lend us their strength. Pray they guide our paths that we might do them and our people honor."

My stomach pains as he wanders into the circle.

"Tonight we dance and feast." Creek Jumper's voice rises. "Tomorrow, we walk the warpath."

Our people offer another onslaught of joyous cries.

The drums bang anew, louder.

My stomach retches with empty hunger. My head swoons with delirium, my vision altering black and red as I sway.

"These four have provided gifts for such favors," says Creek Jumper. "Let others come also and make their offerings. Come... Come!"

Still the drums speak to me. Their beat calling...

Calling...

Calling...

I rise to answer.

The earth tilts.

I keep my feet and resign myself to the music.

Dance. The drums command me. *Dance...Dance...*

Committing my body to their bidding, I circle the fire and feel its heat upon my brow and the cold to my back. My body aches with bliss, even as I fight to keep my balance. I offer up my voice, singing the old songs. The drums and dance are all that matter until the striking pole looms before me, surrounded in shadow.

Fear swells within me, says I am unworthy to strike the pole as the men and even Ciquenackqua did.

The voice of Numees whispers I am an odd squaw, reminds me what my place should be.

Buried in the wood, Father's tomahawk calls to me.

Strike the pole. The drums command. *Strike...Strike...*

My spirit lifts. I dance toward the striking pole and reach for the weapon.

A memory rises within me from the life before—Sarah leaping into the night sky. She falls and crushes Hecate, her legs and joints snapping. Anger washes over me at her disapproval of my claim that I, too, would make such a sacrifice to save my family.

My song becomes a savage scream.

I pluck Father's weapon free of its wooden sheath then bury it over and again, striking in vain attempts to silence the fear and doubt crippling my mind.

"*Rebecca!*"

Father's voice pulls me from the trance.

The drums play no longer. The flickering flames behind me the sole voice I hear.

I look round the circle and find familiar faces unable to meet my gaze.

Even Numees looks on me as a stranger.

Father studies my face as one concerned, though he says nothing.

"She is a fearsome squaw." Two Ravens breaks the quiet. "And near chopped the striking pole in two."

Creek Jumper approaches me warily. "What caused you to rise in such a stupor?" he asks.

"The drums...they bid me rise," I say in earnest.

"Did they bid you scream also?"

"No. I-I saw..."

"Tell me, young one," says Creek Jumper. "What did you see?"

I think of Sarah and feel my eyes sting with tears. "I-I saw death...great sacrifice..." My chest heaves as Creek Jumper lays his hands gently upon my shoulders. "F-forgive me. I did not mean to—"

"Peace, child," he says. "One does not strike the pole in such a way if the ancestors did not grant them a powerful vision."

"But it were a memory I saw," I say. "No vision."

Our shaman seems to weigh my words before turning toward the people. "It is known women have no place in war, but when the ancestors speak, the people must listen."

Those in our tribe nod in acknowledgement of his claim. Then Creek Jumper squints at me. His look sends cold shivers through me as if he peered into my soul and found it lacking.

"I see one before me who has suffered great loss. A darkness long kept, awaiting release," he says. "I say the ancestors speak through Black Pilgrim's daughter this night, and now leave the decision to us."

"What decision?" Whistling Hare asks.

Creek Jumper stares into my eyes. "They mean her to guide us in this battle. Where her fate leads, so too does the people's."

"But she is barely a woman," says Ciquenackqua. "And white also."

I bristle at his words, but keep my silence.

"This world is filled with many colors," says Creek Jumper. "Do you doubt the Creator's design?"

Ciquenackqua hangs his head.

"I do not," says Creek Jumper. "But I am one voice and the people have many. They will decide."

I know not how to react upon seeing those familiar to me nodding.

Deep River's smile swells confidence in me, and I am not a little surprised to see Ciquenackqua's face darken as his father claps me on the shoulder and squeezes.

"I would gladly go to war with such a warrior as she." Whistling Hare looks to Father. "Would you, brother?"

Father says nothing for what feels an eternity. Then, slowly, he nods.

I fight to keep myself rooted to the ground as the whoops and war cries sound anew.

Another hand touches upon my shoulder, bids me look on his white-painted face and red tears.

"She cannot go without knowing the face of her *manitous,*" says Creek Jumper.

"But it has not yet revealed itself," I say.

Creek Jumper's eyes shine. "Your vision has already begun, else you could not have pulled the weapon from the striking pole. Your *manitous* lent you strength in that moment. Now, we will ask that it reveal its form to you."

-six-

Creek Jumper leads me away from the bonfire.

My steps stutter, and I lean upon his arm for guidance as hunger threatens to whisk me into the dream fast.

He directs me to the sweat lodge and pulls back the buckskin flap that I might enter first. A wave of heat slaps me the moment I step inside, waking me to my new surroundings.

Though fairly bare of ornament, I find the lodge comforting. The fire's orange hues and crackling wood emote the sense I am in my own home. Skins of water and various ingredients line the wall—tobacco, cedar, and a strange bowl filled with purplish-black powder—all of which Creek Jumper will offer to the flames as my firekeeper.

The stones pulse warmth into the air as my muscles fail, begging me to sleep. Their heat forces me to sit upon a bison hide. I lean to lie down.

"No, child." Creek Jumper halts me. "Patience."

He remains with me until I am steady. Only then does he leave my side and cross to the wall. He takes up a skin of water and mutters ancient prayers as he pours the contents atop the heating stones.

The stones sizzle and hiss, their angry steam filling the lodge.

Creek Jumper shows me that I must drink deep of their heat, call the steam into my body with sweeping waves of my arms.

I follow his example, and feel my body warmed from the inside.

He kneels and takes up the strange bowl. Sprinkles its blackish powder into the fire.

A new scent seeps into my nostrils, smelling of both sweet grass and honey.

My muscles relax as Creek Jumper takes a seat upon his bison hide. He holds a small drum, crafted from the hollowed shell of a painted turtle. Gently, he shakes the handle.

"Listen, child." Creek Jumper says to me. "Heed the call."

I close my eyes, and listen to the stones and bones rebounding inside the drum.

Creek Jumper begins to sing, his words soothing, lulling me into blissful sleep.

Then I feel something new, liken to insects crawling up my arms and legs.

I reach to brush them aside.

It serves only to hasten their speed.

I shout for Creek Jumper to aid me.

His song deepens, drowning out my cries. His drum beats louder, faster.

My skin feels aflame. I scratch at it. My nails dig deep, yet they cannot reach the pain. My eyes open wide to Creek Jumper's painted face and tears.

"Listen, child," he again commands. "Heed the call."

The heat suffocates me. Begs me to leave this hellish place and dip myself in cool waters.

Instead, I close my eyes and fight the urge, homing on Creek Jumper's song and the beat of his drum. My body sways with ecstatic fever then I pitch forward into darkness.

ೲ

I sprint through the underbrush, hurdling over rocks and fallen limbs, chasing my quarry by the light of the moon.

My prey titters above me and leaps from branch to branch. It leads me further into the woods. The trickster of the forest does not fear me like his woodland cousins. He knows patience and believes his taunts and high position are like to frustrate me into forfeiting my chase.

But I am not so easily thwarted. I pursue with little sense of passing time, or where my prey leads. Only when my legs threaten to give out does the animal stop and mock me again with its chatter.

I gaze high into the darkened treetops. My target eludes my sight, for now, though I know he yet abides over me.

Hiding. Waiting.

I nock my arrow and stare upward, awaiting any movement, or the reflective glint of the animal's eyes.

The brush beside me moves. A shadow steps forward.

"Father..."

The chill in the air grants life to his breath. He shifts his gaze upward, squints.

The old ones in our tribe oft mention their belief Father possesses the night sight, a gift given him by the owl feathers he wears in his hair.

Father whistles like a dove of the morning might, then slowly raises his hand. Again, he would prove the old ones correct this night, spotting the creature before I do.

I follow his point.

A pair of glittering eyes stares back at me from behind its natural black mask. The raccoon steps further into the light and perches on the slightest of branches, daring me take my shot.

I pull the bowstring taut near my ear. Breathing in the October cold, I wait for the animal to give me some little signal its spirit has readied to leave this world.

It gives me no such sign.

My eyes squint in wonder at its fearlessness, and I wonder what manner of creature so willfully stares down its hunter.

The muscles in my forearm twitch. My legs and back ache, begging me release my stance.

My arrow does not fly.

Wind breezes past, kisses my cheeks with chilling caress. It hails from the northeast.

Faintly, the wind whispers.

Something comes…

Father places a hand on my shoulder, drawing my attention.

I find his appearance altered. Gone are his long locks and owl feathers, his head now shorn. A living demon crafted in twilight, save for the whites of his eyes.

Like the blood trail of a wounded animal, traces of sappy darkness remain on my shoulder as Father withdraws his hand. I gather the blackness coating his body comes not from ash or paint even before I touch it. Indeed, the residue feels warm, liken to tree sap, and stains my skin.

I glance up and see Father's cheeks draw tight.

He seems hardly to breathe at all as we wait, listening for any sign the forest might give of that to come, any ill spirit that shares our hunting grounds this eve.

Then, more than whispers.

Slow and rhythmic, their beat falls steady as the spring rains on the home I share with Father and Sarah.

Drums. Their sound hails from the direction of our village. I grimace, knowing the time for rain dances have come and gone…

"Father," I whisper. "What gives the grandfathers cause to bang the drums?"

He does not appear to have heard me at all. His vision shifts to the treetops and my prey as the gay sound of pipes emerge from deeper in the forest.

A shadow falls from the sky, shrieking, its mouth agape, eyes wild.

I whip my bow up. My string *twangs,* and a *whoosh* of air breezes near my cheek.

My arrow flies wide of the target.

The snarling beast lands atop my head, collapses me with its weight. Biting and clawing, its shrill voice fills my ears.

I swat at the moving mass of muscle and fur. My fingers clutch around its tail. I yank it free and its nails rend my scalp in reward.

Growling, the raccoon seeks a new handhold.

Its claws call fresh blood from my forearms. I fight the urge to scream, and give the beast little chance to find deeper purchase. Swinging it free, I release the animal into the night.

Limbs crack as it lands in the distance.

Pain flows from thin scratches the raccoon left me with, all of them oozing blood. Wetness dampens my brow.

I brush the stickiness away with my hands. Both come away spackled crimson-black. My limbs falter, and I kneel for balance as the unseen drums and flutes play on.

I blink away the blood dripping in my eyes, and notice Father watching me.

A shadow of Sarah's voice reminds me his name is Priest.

But I find no benevolence in giving the man before me such a name. Indeed, witnessing Father in the cruel torchlight, I think it easier to understand how the natives named him Black Pilgrim. A worthy name to honor a formidable adversary, or so Bishop told me in the stories of my youth. I recall, even then, wishing I, too, could earn such a formidable name.

Now, I am uncertain.

Father stares down at me, much the same as the ringed-tail had from its lofty perch. Yet where the animal glared at me in malicious wonder, far worse lives in Father's gaze.

Disappointment.

"Father," I say. "Why did you not come to my aid?"

His silence angers me more than my open wounds.

I rise and feel another dizzy spell force me to earth again.

"Father..." I mutter.

Still, he makes no effort to visit me. Indeed, he turns to leave.

Fire rages in my spirit. Grunting, I fight to stand, closing my eyes to keep from falling once more.

"Father!" I call.

I reopen my eyes and find him halted.

I stumble closer to join him.

The world threatens to spin beneath me if I continue.

"Father...why did you not—"

I stop short upon seeing he holds a blade in his left hand—the same dagger I have often gazed upon many a time. The same weapon Sarah used to slay Hecate, the Devil's daughter, and save our family in the life before.

With a flick of his wrist, Father throws the blade at my feet. Even in darkness, I know the name etched upon its blade—*Captain John Alden, Jr.* A family weapon passed down from father to bastard son, now embedded in the dirt between my legs.

I pluck it free and hold its tip aloft as Father vanishes into the thicket.

The dizziness cripples me.

"Father, don't!" I cry. "Don't leave me."

The wind howls, burying my plea, yet even it cannot silence the flutes and drums. Only after the wind dissipates does something stir from inside the wood.

My hand quivering, I reach for a nearby elm to steady myself.

"Father…" I say. When he does not reappear, I call out with the name my sister gives him. "*Priest…*come back…"

My wounds throb in warning the noisemaker is not he, even as I call for him.

Small in stature, ferocious in nature, the noisemaker reveals itself to me.

The raccoon pauses in a ray of moonlight. Its head cocks to the side, studying me. Then it growls.

Your father is gone. I gather the animal's meaning. *As is the man Priest. Only the Black Pilgrim remains…and you are no daughter to him. He has no family.*

I point the shaking dagger tip in the raccoon's direction.

The animal opens its mouth, hisses.

"C-come for me, s-spirit," I say, my body suddenly weak as the dizziness returns to claim me. "I-I would learn what gift you would lend me."

My knees buckle. I fall to earth, my face plastered in mud.

Ravens caw overhead.

I glance up.

A pair of the dark messengers descends from their perches. They settle near the raccoon, flanking the ringed-tail on either side.

I wonder what strange lesson the grandfathers mean for me to learn as the ravens jabber at one another.

The raccoon hisses them silent, its beady gaze upon me. It leaves the birds and scuttles toward me.

My limbs refuse to move, bound to the cold mud by an unseen force. I force myself to stare at the raccoon, and await its claws to finish the job it began on my face.

The animal halts a few inches from me. Sitting on its haunches, it strokes its whiskers with tiny paws and looks on me curiously, then opens its mouth.

"Waken…" The raccoon's voice sounds gravelly and raw, as if the earth itself opened to speak with me.

My eyes widen.

The raccoon ambles before me, holds me with its gaze. "*Waken, child.*"

Strong hands grip my shoulders and break the enchantment cast over my limbs. They pull me to a seated position.

My eyes flutter open.

The raccoon has vanished. So too have the ravens and the woods.

I look to my forearms and observe no scratches. No blood or black stains of the residue that coated Father's body. Even the feeling of insects and inflammation has vanished. Now my skin feels damp and clammy, sweat-ridden.

A guiding hand forces me to take hold of the leather water skin thrust into my open palms.

"Drink," Creek Jumper commands, though not unkindly.

I guzzle the tepid water, draining the skin. Slowly, my strength returns.

Creek Jumper shuffles behind me. Wood slaps against leather and coolness saps the heat and haze from the sweat lodge.

The firelight wanes. Its tips flicker, threatening to flee if the breeze continues.

The flap door closes, and the fire blooms anew.

Creek Jumper moves slow and sure round the fire. The clinking of beads and bone from the leather pouch around his neck comforts that no evil spirit may take me in his presence.

The firelight dances between us. It casts our long shadows against the far wall as Creek Jumper again takes his seat upon the bison hide.

"What vision did the ancestors grant you, child?" he asks.

His face remains a stone as I recount my vision. Indeed, he shows me little sign he is to have heard my tale at all. Only when I finish does he give me the smallest of nods.

"Even the wisest cannot know all that the *manitous* reveals in the dream fast," said Creek Jumper. "For some, the visions come to bear soon. Others..." He shakes his head.

"Aye," I say. "But what do you believe of mine? What message would they have me understand? Learn what lesson?"

Creek Jumper palms a handful of softened corn from his bowl. Eats the kernels slowly, all while staring into the fire.

"Fear is the message." His eyes narrow at me. "Slaying it the lesson."

"I do not understand," I say.

"Your *manitous* is a curious one." Creek Jumper palms another handful of corn.

"Aye," I say, my thought dwelling on the raccoon. "How can it be the grandfathers would have me follow such a dishonest spirit?"

Creek Jumper sighs. "Trickery...deception...two of many masks the ringed-tail wears. Do not mistake them for an evil nature. Honor instead this creature's cunning and resourceful ways. Learn to wear all the masks it would teach you."

I nod in acknowledgement of his words, even if I do not understand them. "And what of my father?" I ask. "Why would I witness his body blackened? Why would he leave me, unaided?"

"To fear his loss marks a good father. You have felt it before."

"I do not recall that other man." I say, struggling to keep my temper. "And the book my sister gives me teaches he was greedy of gain at the expense of others. Is it wrong that I do not mourn the loss of such an evil man?"

"Good and evil," says Creek Jumper. "Both masks we assign others to wear at our choosing. Black Pilgrim decided we march the warpath this morning. Some might call him good for such an act. Others would say it evil."

"But he would seek vengeance on those who have wronged others."

"Others we do not know," says Creek Jumper. "Nor ever will. They walk the spirit path now. We have only the words of Two Ravens."

I think before speaking, wondering what Creek Jumper would teach me. The answer comes to me at seeing the red-painted tears upon his cheeks. "You do not trust him..."

Creek Jumper's face breaks in his own quiet way. "Say instead that I am cautious," he says. "As is Black Pilgrim."

"But you...you made the war dance."

"I performed a shaman's rites," says Creek Jumper. "My role among the people says I must carry the offerings others would give. And so I follow our warriors into battle that I might lend my talents and see our men return."

"And Father?" I ask. "Why would he follow a man he does not trust into battle?"

Creek Jumper reaches for the last of his corn. "When the grandfathers granted me a vision of my own *manitous,* I saw grizzlies upon the rock at the river mouth, fetching salmon as each fish leapt from the water. One survived its hunters and continued its course. When I woke from the dream fast, I went to my father. 'Why did the fish risk the long claws?' I asked him. 'Would it not have been safer for them to stay deep and safe?"

Our shaman chews his corn thoughtfully, lost in his own memories. Only after he swallows the corn does he speak again.

"My father said if the salmon did not follow, the fish would never know what lay upstream. That to not follow its path made the fish dead already."

I think on his words awhile. "Father is curious then..."

Creek Jumper nods.

"It is not like him to make such a hasty decision," I say. "If he were only curious, he would go alone to discover more. Father would not risk our warriors if he did not think it of grave importance." I look to Creek Jumper, concern plaguing my every word. "What was said in the longhouse to convince him?"

Creek Jumper's jaw works back and forth, and I gather him weighing his thoughts. He sighs at the last.

"Your father gave permission for you to journey with us,"

says Creek Jumper. "A rite not granted all women. Only women who have lost one they hold dear and receive a vision may march the warpath."

I open my mouth to tell Creek Jumper I have lost no such person.

He halts me with a raised hand. "It is right that you know what was discussed, since the answer also lies with you and your sister."

My throat catches in wonder of what he speaks.

"Eat." Creek Jumper gives me a bit of dried jerky. "And stay. I will return."

He ambles toward the leather flap and opens it.

The sky shades violet with the approaching dawn. The sight surprises me. I had not thought of the dream fast holding me for so long.

I gnaw on the jerky, my mind hurrying me to make ready for the warpath with Father and the other braves. I fight the urge, reminding myself that Father would not leave without me and that I must first learn what Creek Jumper would teach.

His return comes swiftly. He clutches a gift, wrapped in the same bundled fox pelt he took from the council longhouse.

Creek Jumper sits next to me on the bison hide and sets the gift between us.

I desire to reach for the pelt, and uncover what secret it holds. Instead, I look to our shaman. Observe he too looks upon the pelt.

"Your father and I have spoken much about the events bringing you all here," he says. "Black Pilgrim warned of the hate that powerful white men had for him and your family. He said he would not have their anger fall on us for sheltering you."

Creek Jumper grins.

"I told him powerful white men have long hated our people," he says.

The silence between us worries me. "You think these men… the Mathers." I recall the names from the Putnam journal my sister keeps. "You believe they search for us now?"

A low rumble rises in Creek Jumper's throat as he sits in reflective study.

"Two Ravens said he and his men returned to the raided village," Creek Jumper says of a sudden. "Bodies lay where they fell, untouched, still bearing jewelry and weapons."

My hopes rise. "Then the raiders cannot have been white men. They take all they can carry."

"We share the same mind," says Creek Jumper.

I think back on the previous night and all Two Ravens had said about the rumors. I well remember his scorn for me. "What of the white women?" I ask. "He said they, too, fought."

Creek Jumper shakes his head. "That did not sway us."

"Then what convinced Father?" I ask.

Creek Jumper reaches for the fox pelt.

My breath catches as he pulls back the flap.

A crude, bone-hilted dagger lay at the center of the pelt. The base of it is carved into a skull with two strings, one black, the other red, tied from either eye socket. They run down its cheeks as if the skull weeps colors.

I stare upon its familiar blade and recall many nights at Bishop's side, listening to his tales of leprechauns, banshees, and witches.

"You know this blade?" Creek Jumper asks.

"The one I name grandfather owns its twin. He tells a story

of the ribbons' meaning." I take the dagger in hand, staring at its handle and the ribbons draped from its eyes. "Red for the innocence stolen from them. Black for the histories that darken their names."

I look into Creek Jumper's eyes.

"It's Salem's vengeance."

Confusion masks his face.

"The powerful white men." I say. "They leave the blades as a warning."

Creek Jumper grunts as he takes the dagger from my hands. "Then we will find these white men and their warrior women." He rips the red and black ribbons from the eye sockets then tosses both into the fire. "And leave our own warning."

-seven-

THE MORNING SUN PEEKS OVER THE HORIZON AS I LEAVE THE sweat lodge. It has banished most of the stars, but a few yet remain to shine upon me.

I look upon them and offer a silent prayer to the ancestors, thanking them for the vision, asking they lend me courage on the warpath.

A mound of glowing embers stands where the towering bonfire did when last I saw it. Trampled grass encircles the ashy remainder, signaling the many feet that made the war dance, and the striking pole leans heavy with several deep gashes.

My mind wonders what took hold of me last eve to grant such strength.

The flap opens behind me as Creek Jumper leaves the sweat lodge. He breathes deep of the morning air, his nose wrinkling as he looks on me.

"Go to the river," he says. "Cleanse yourself. It would not do for your smell to give us away."

I smile back at him then take my leave. Along the way, cook fires burn, babies cry, and an occasional brave steps from his home to relieve himself.

The signs of my village stirring hasten my step through the palisade opening. I head east toward the riverbank, watching the first rays of sunlight sparkle on the water.

A noise from inside the woods, liken to a fawn frightened

from its resting place, halts me. The sound does not drive deeper into the forest like an animal should, nor does it grow quiet like a startled person might. Instead the sound continues, thrashing.

I draw my long dagger. My pulse quickens as I enter the thicket, soundless and sure as Father taught me. I do not travel far before discovering the noise source.

Spinning and stumbling, Ciquenackqua dances around a weak fire.

I crouch behind an old oak in silent watch.

Three times Ciquenackqua dances around the fire before I understand he means to imitate Father's movements, but he has not yet mastered control of his body. His feet do not lift in time and he near trips himself.

He stops and kicks the ground, frustration crossing his face. I think to laugh, and remind him he is not yet such a renowned brave.

The thought vanishes when he sits hard upon the ground and puts his face in his hands, his back shuddering.

My mind reminds me pity is for the weak.

My spirit reaches out to one who would practice the war dance alone, as I often have. Shame washes over me that I should witness such a private act.

I rise from my position, and creep away so that he will not hear.

I sprint for the riverbank after emerging from the woods.

Our overturned canoes line the shore. I grin at the sight of them and revel at the thought I will soon share one with Father, the pair of us riding the stream downriver with the other men.

I slip off my moccasins and wade into the frigid water, stopping when it reaches my knees.

Small fish scatter as I enter their domain, clouding their home.

I bend low and dip my hands. I palm handfuls of sand into them then scrub my arms, neck, and face until all feel raw and flush red. I wonder what the warpath holds for me. What it must feel like to take a man's life. If I will hesitate at the killing time, or commit the act as Father would have me do.

The cold seeps into my skin, a reminder I should not linger. Already, braves head toward the canoes carrying dried meat, robes, and weapons.

Splashing myself clean, I hurry back to the shore and fetch my moccasins. I run to our village and round the palisades to find our village thrives with braves gathering their things and saying their goodbyes.

The flurry of activity catches me as well. I waste no time in sprinting for my home.

Numees and Deep River pass me along the way. She opens her mouth as if she would speak.

Instead, Deep River ushers her stay with him.

I gather that I have missed something, but continue on my way.

The surrounding noise lessens as I yank back the flap and enter my home.

Sarah sits beside the fire, her Bible lying open in her lap. She glances up, her eyes red with tears. "Did Priest find you?"

I dislike the tone of her question. One that warns I will like her reasoning behind it even less. "No," I reply. "I have not seen him since the dancing fire. Why do you ask?"

Sarah looks again on her Bible. "He and I spoke much after his decision. All night, in truth."

I think back at how Numees looked on me and what her face said that she could not bring herself to speak, nor Deep River allow her to.

"You would talk him from it," I say. "Ask him not to make war on the Iroquois?"

"No," she says. "He is a war chief. His duty calls him to protect the people. I could not sway him from such a task, even if I desired it more than anything else in the world. And to change his decision now would make him seem weak."

"Then what decision do you speak of?" I ask.

Sarah wavers before answering me, casting her gaze to earth. "I asked him renounce his claim for your company on the warpath."

Anger swarms within me at Sarah's answer. My jaw works wordlessly as unpleasant thoughts seethe in my mind. "How... how could he...why would you—"

"Must you ask? Truly?" Sarah says, tears welling in her eyes. "I love you, sister. With all my heart."

I fall to my knees. "Then why would you do this? You know better than any what such a decision means to me. He honored me in front of our people by granting permission."

"They are not my people, Rebecca." Sarah scoots toward me, taking hold of my hands. "*You* are, sweet sister. Shadows that you both may be in this home, you and my husband are all I have left in this cruel world. I could not bear to lose you both."

I pull my hands back from hers. "You speak untruths, Sarah. You have George also—"

"No," she says. "Our brother has not come here in many a year now. Not since his own children died from the pox."

I sneer at her words. "Or perhaps he comes no more since

you told him our family is cursed. That its dark magic fell even upon on his children."

"We *are* cursed, Rebecca." Sarah insists. "Outcast. How can it be you and George will not see? God forces us to wander in the wilderness for our sins."

"I do not wander," I say. "Father taught me all the secrets of the forest. Showed me the goodly spirits that reside in all things. He would show you also, but you will not see them. You would rather cower in a hut."

Sarah looks away from me. "My legs—"

"Fear cripples you." I spit. "Nothing more. Creek Jumper could heal your legs if only you believed."

"I know not what to believe anymore, sister." Sarah closes her Bible. "Do you think I do not feel the anger in your heart? I do. It lives in mine also."

"Do not speak of my anger," I say. "What could you know of it?"

"You think my soul does not rage, Rebecca? You cry I withhold that which you desire more than anything. You, who know better than most what *I* have lost? Family...a husband's love... the simple joy of running through the woods."

My sister flings her Bible across the hut, startling me.

"Everything I hold dear turns to dust!" she shrieks.

I know not what to say as Sarah looks on me with a wildness I have never before seen in her. She cups her face with her hands, shaking and sobbing.

"F-forgive me, sister," Sarah says. "I fear our mother passed on her madness to me. But all that I did, all that I do...it is to keep you safe with me."

I do little to hide the disdain in my face as she looks on me.

"I do not question your love for me, Sarah, or that you would know I am safe from harm," I say. "But you did not do all for that alone."

"What do you say?"

"You would keep me here to wallow with you," I say. "Speaking endlessly of curses and witchery, but you can yet live, Sarah."

"You mock me." Sarah snorts.

I kneel next to her, and take her hands again in mine.

"No!"

She shrinks, clutching her head as if she berates herself in ways I cannot know or hear. She looks upon me, wiping tears from her eyes.

"It is too late for me, sister," Sarah says, touching my cheek.

I draw away. "It is not for me. Let me go and find Priest. You swayed him from his decision already. Let you convince him now. Ask that I may go—"

Sarah shakes her head. "I have seen enough death to last me all the rest of my days. Our mother and father killed, and my dearest friends also. So many years ago, and still their faces haunt my dreams each night." She takes my hand in hers and kisses the backs of them. "Do not begrudge my desire to keep you safe."

I turn stony as my sister wipes her tears away. I leave her side and gather my things—bow and arrows, my winter robes, and a bag of corn for the journey.

"I know you are angry with me." Sarah's words halt me ere I leave. "And I will wear that proudly, knowing it keeps you well. I ask you grant me one kindness only."

"What?"

"Do not..." Her voice breaks. "Do not let your anger for me turn hateful."

Not wishing to lie, I leave our hut without giving the answer she seeks.

The village has near emptied as I run through it. Only a few of the old ones sit outside their homes, some nibbling on soft corn, others gambling on their bowl games.

My people gather outside the palisades, forcing me to thread my way through them. More of our braves dip their canoes into the river, while all who came with Two Ravens have already pushed off downstream.

I pass Numees, locked in Deep River's embrace, and search the faces of those not yet in their canoes. Father is nowhere to be seen.

I shield my eyes, squint to learn if he cast off with Whistling Hare and Ciquenackqua.

Creek Jumper is last to leave our shores, sharing a canoe with his son. Our shaman offers tobacco to the water panther in request the spirit not drown our men.

My people shout and wave as the braves dip their oars.

Anger and grief forbid my soul from adding my voice to theirs.

"Rebecca."

Sturdy Oak stands behind me, his wispy white hair blowing in the breeze.

"Come," he bids. "Speak with me."

As our people walk back to the village, I follow our peace chief toward the Swinging Tree. On any other day, the willowy branches would call my name to climb them and dive from their heights. Today, even the gentle song of their rustling leaves brings me no comfort.

Sturdy Oak sits beneath the tree, bidding me sit beside him. He lights the *calumet* and puffs it. A series of smoke circles leave his lips, expanding as they ascend.

We sit in quiet for what seems to me a long while. Only when I fear my silence will no longer keep does he speak.

"You are angry with your father," he says.

"Should I not be?" I ask. "Glory is given to those who make the warpath. I would make my father proud. Bring him the honor he deserves."

"Then trust his judgment."

"But he said I could go, Grandfather."

Sturdy Oak says nothing for a time, and I fear he will never speak. Still, I remain at his side, smelling the tobacco smoke he exhales, waiting for his words.

"It is right that you are angry with Black Pilgrim," he says finally. "You have lost much to these warrior women he would fight, but those who have lost much must cling to what little remains."

"You speak of my sister."

He nods. "You are still young and know not the happiness of a husband and children. Other times, the burden." Sturdy Oak puffs the *calumet*. "We are a generous people, but we would not have taken any strangers among us if we had not sensed goodness in them, a love of family and the will to protect them at all costs. I recognized such love when first our paths crossed in the woods those many years ago."

Sturdy Oak passes me the *calumet*, and smiles as one lost in his memories.

"You will not remember this, for you were still young that day," he says. "But I think on it often. Some counseled we should not trust white folk and, when the others decided to kill your family, I said nothing against it."

My breath catches in my throat at his words.

Sturdy Oak hangs his head. "You are right to be surprised, for it shames me to say I agreed with them. Though my role forbids it, hate lingered in my heart at the death of my son to white traders."

"But we are still here," I say. "What stayed their hands?"

"You." Sturdy Oak chuckles at my confusion and takes back the *calumet*. "In truth, they stopped at my bidding," he says. "But it was the sight of you and Black Pilgrim that swayed me."

"I don't understand."

"He knew we lingered in the woods, surrounding your camp," says Sturdy Oak. "I expected him to attack us, or move close to your sister, who I thought he favored."

"He did not?"

Sturdy Oak shakes his head. "He stood between us and you, blocking your sight from us as if he would spare you the sight of death." Sturdy Oak clears his throat. "A father will sacrifice all, even his own soul, to protect his child. When I saw this white stranger's love for you that day, it banished hate in my heart for then and always. I saw in him a man I would proudly name son and asked him become mine in place of the one I lost."

"Why do you tell me this?" I ask.

"Black Pilgrim looks on you proudly as his daughter."

The ice around my heart thaws with his mention. I think of Father just so, smiling on me after my first kill, and again when I slew the mountain lion that would have taken his life.

"But he also calls your sister his wife," Sturdy Oak says. "And it is right he sides with her against you in this matter."

Anger rises within me at his words. "How can you speak so, Grandfather?" I ask. "He spoke untruths when he left me behind."

Sturdy Oak shakes his head. "Black Pilgrim said you would make the war path and so you do."

"But I am here."

"Along with many others." He motions toward our village. "Do we that remain sacrifice less? Those who go have knowledge of who returns and who does not. We that stay must wait and wonder."

I hang my head in shame as he continues.

"Those who die are gone," he says. "We others must wait to join them on the spirit path. You will find both trails hard to walk, but know old men like me take comfort your bow and knife guards us."

I look up. "What say you?"

"You think glory is given to those who leave, and you are right," says Sturdy Oak. "It goes also to those who protect the people. Black Pilgrim honors us by leaving his daughter as a guardian."

His words bring me some small comfort as I look on the river. The canoes are but specks to my eyes, and still I wish my place among them. Sturdy Oak's words are not lost on me, but I should rather be with them and experience the war path.

I sit with Sturdy Oak a long while, listening to the rustling leaves and river song.

My mind wanders to Sarah and the ill words I left her with. The thought that I may have split she and Father shames me, though I cannot bring myself to rise and go to her. My anger yet swirls, despite Sturdy Oak's kindness.

I finger the string of my bow. Listen to it *twang* upon my release.

"The woods have ever been a place of solace," says Sturdy Oak. "Let you go and visit them now. A long hunt would do your spirit good."

I smile at the notion, and rise to leave. Slinging my bow and quiver, robes and corn meal, I sprint for the forest and listen to the wind in my ears. I crash into the wilderness, allowing its power to sink into me. My feet run without knowing where they lead, though my mind knows what I hunt for.

A single thought keeps me.

I will find my *manitous* and learn what lessons it will teach me.

My search leads me deep into the woods. A full two days and nights I search 'round the perimeter of my village, hunting for my *manitous,* finding traces—scratched bark, droppings—but never catching sight of a ringed-tail.

The third morn's approaching dawn bids me give up my search. Hunting the raccoon in the early hour would do little good, they being nightwalkers. I do not bother drafting a fire, instead retiring to the sleeping robes I carry slung over my shoulder.

The vision granted me in the dream fast returns no sooner than I fall asleep. Again, I see Father's face, covered in pitch, as he leaves me to the raccoon and the ravens.

I wake near afternoon and begin the walk back, finding my return journey pleasant. I dwell on the words of Sturdy Oak. His mention of spending time in the woods alone bids me wonder if Father's frequent disappearances into their midst occurred for similar reasons.

I think on the war party as twilight falls. They should have reached the trading post days ago if they stuck to the river. I wonder if they halted and spent the evening with George and the others.

I dismiss the notion.

Father would not wish any in his company given over to firewater. I think rather they should stop on the return from war to celebrate their victory.

My mind warns no victory is certain in war.

Just as the thought puts fear in my heart, a familiar titter calls from the trees.

I kneel to earth. Wrap a bit of dry moss around a stick then strike my flint.

The spark catches.

I stand again, lift my torch high, and cast my gaze skyward.

The reflective glow in the raccoon's eyes signal me.

It dashes off to the next branch before I unsling my bow. I race after it, listening to its chatter, allowing its taunts to feed my spirit with strength to carry on the hunt.

Several times over, I think it doubles back on its trail, attempting to throw me. Still, I hold true to my course, homing on the sound of rustling leaves and branches, even when I lose sight of my quarry.

Always I look to the sky and stars for my bearings, as Father taught me. The ringed-tail leads me toward my village, and I recognize the landscape for my father's hunting grounds.

The ringed-tail halts and I pause to catch my breath, panting as I keep my gaze locked on the treetop where last I saw the animal.

The raccoon again makes itself known, perching at the end of a limb.

The eyes behind its black mask send shivers down my spine, reminding me of my vision. I unsling my bow and nock an arrow.

Still the animal does not move.

The muscles in my forearm quiver, begging me release the arrow.

A shadow leaps from the forest, knocking me astray.

My arrow flies wide, and my attention wheels to the snarling beast atop me. Long, stringy hair fills my mouth, and I smell the stench of an unwashed person.

The torchlight provides a glimpse of my attacker—a young woman.

Her face bears scabs and scratches, some fresh with blood, picked at recently. She holds a cruel bone-dagger in hand. Two ribbons—black and red—dangle from its skull hilt.

Witch! A memory of the life before screams the word at me.

She raises her dagger and screeches at me, her breath putrid even from afar.

I draw my long knife and plunge its tip deep through her left armpit, twisting it at the last, as I would a wounded animal.

The witch's scream dies in her throat as she falls off me.

My hands clammy, I withdraw the dagger and find my feet again. I grab up my torch and see the lit end quiver.

I cast my gaze to the forest searching for anyone else meaning me harm.

I spy nothing.

Hear nothing.

I turn the torch's light upon the dead witch and note her garment worn and black. The hood she wore has fallen off, spilling a tangled mess of brown hair. Her face bears the look of one not yet a woman, barely a girl. Purplish-black powder stains her nostrils, almost as if she bled it.

Looking on her dead face, I realize she is my first kill. I think on Sarah, the guilt she speaks of holding to this day for Hecate's death.

I feel nothing for the witch before me. Pride, if anything, that I fought her off.

My eyes fall again on the dagger she meant to slay me with.

"This is how they mark the houses." I whisper words from the life before.

I look upward and find the raccoon still perched above, watching me.

My mind wonders if the animal lured me here in ambush as even Creek Jumper acknowledged my *manitous* a tricksome spirit.

I look on the dead witch again, wonder what other lesson might be learned.

The raccoon turns its head north.

I follow its gaze to rising pillars of smoke.

Shouts and screams echo across the night sky.

"No..."

The raccoon leaps to the next branch, bound for the screaming and the smoke.

Bound for my village.

-eight-

I SPRINT THROUGH THE FOREST, HEADED FOR THE ORANGE PLUMES of light that brighten with each passing moment and make the forest glow.

War cries fill my ears as I near my village. I hunker behind a tree to survey the situation.

Few canoes remain upon the shore and near all aflame.

A pair of braves guard our entrance, their hair styled in Mohawk manner. Faces scarred and scratched. Picked at.

They catch the women and children of my tribe who try to flee, killing any who fight them.

My hand flies to my quiver. I nock an arrow and aim then let it fly.

The arrowhead finds a home in the first brave's throat. He falls clutching its feathers, gasping as his partner searches for the source.

His mistake is to not look toward the forest.

My second arrow fells him in likewise manner.

I draw both my long dagger and tomahawk. I rush toward the entrance, leaping over the fallen bodies in my path, shutting my eyes to their faces, not wishing to know who lies among the slain.

I veer right once inside, and hide behind the first hut I find.

Panic swirls as my village burns. Everywhere those familiar to me flee. Boys try their hands against seasoned warriors, the bravest of them felled quickly. The others are disarmed, forced to the ground, and bound.

One woman walks tall among the rest, garbed in animal skins. Unlike the hooded witches flanking her every side, she wears a pelt upon her head. The dead animal's nose and mouth descending into the line of black painted across her eyes.

She halts in the open field, and welcomes two of our men to battle. She takes both head on, striking and screaming as her long knives search for new ways to paint their blades red.

Both braves fall under her, and she finishes them in a screeching bloodlust.

My spirits wishes to engage her.

My mind bids otherwise.

A group of captives sit tied at the gathering circle where we performed the war dance. Some hang their heads in shame. Others cry out for aid but receive none.

My anger pulses at the sight, yet I do not stir.

I search the faces of those in the center, hoping not to find Sarah.

My shoulders sag noticing Sturdy Oak among them. Blood drips down his forehead, yet he keeps his pride. His back straight and tall despite the bonds stringing his hands to his feet, willing him break and bend.

Memories of Father's teachings urge I should not linger, that the animal holding its position dies sooner than that which keeps moving.

I slink from hut to hut, progressing ever closer to my own.

Several times, I witness neighbors cast from their homes. Others dragged, bound and gagged, as warriors and hooded women put their huts to the torch.

Every fiber of my being begs me help them, yet I know I should join them as a captive if I do.

I forget all pretenses upon seeing Numees. A pair of braves hold her upon the ground, their positions warning they mean her dishonor.

I fall upon them without thinking, screaming the war cry of our people as my tomahawk and long dagger strike in quick succession. When my vision clears, I find both braves dead beneath me.

"Rebecca." Numees stands, tugs at my arm. "Come…we must go!"

I shrug her off, and turn to the hut I share with Sarah and Father.

Fear takes hold of me. Warns I should not enter.

I plunge inside.

My sister leans on her crutch, a hatchet in hand. Her grim demeanor fades upon seeing me. "Rebecca…I thought you lost."

"Come. Quick—"

A kick in my back sends me hurtling toward the fire.

I roll away from the flames, and bring my blades to bear as a shadow falls upon me. I struggle to fight the brave, the pair of us rolling, wrestling to gain the upper hand.

The brave groans at the thud on his back and he falls limp upon me.

Sarah stands over me, her face pale. "I…I…"

My fingers graze the hilt of my sister's hatchet in the back of the dead brave. I pluck the weapon free and hand it back to Sarah.

She looks on the hatchet hesitantly.

"Take it." I force the handle into her palm then help her out of our hut.

"*Rebecca...*" Numees hisses behind our home. She waves us over.

I throw my sister's arm across my shoulder to steady her. Together, we limp to the back.

"Help me," I say to Numees. "We must carry her."

"Rebecca, no," says Sarah. "Go now. Leave me."

"No." I grit my teeth. "I will not."

"Where will we go?" Numees asks. "The entrance is too far."

My gaze wanders over the palisade. The wooden walls, so long offering protection, have now become my prison. Like hunters herding their quarry, the witches and braves have fenced us in.

"We follow the wall," I say. "It may be they found a weak spot to enter in."

My conscience knows it a false hope, even as I speak the words. Still, I hold fast to the notion the raging fires might well have provided us an escape.

The three of us hobble onward, our heads swiveling in search of any raiders drawing near. Several times, we are forced to endure the sounds of our neighbors dragged away. Angry tears flood my cheeks at each wail.

I try and shut their voices out, attempting instead to focus on my sister and Numees.

Sarah winces at the pace we force upon her. To her credit, she does not falter. Not even when I bid her move faster.

The sounds of struggle wane with each passing moment, while victory cries grow louder. The thought of our last defenses falling encourages me to move faster.

Sarah cannot.

Numees, too, fights exhaustion, and I gather the struggle to maintain her honor weakened her. When she collapses, Sarah and I fall with her.

My sister yelps, her ankle *popping*.

I clap my hand over Sarah's mouth, pull her head close to my chest as her face twists in anguish. I look down the palisade wall and sight a burned section, small enough for a child to fit through.

"Sarah, look." I point to the opening. "We can make it."

I crawl away from her, peeking around the edge of the hut.

The elation I felt dissipates at the warrior striding through the village, his face paint streaked white and black. Atop his head, Two Ravens wears the fuzzy brow of a bison bull, its black horns curve upward, their tips piercing through decapitated raven heads.

Anger course through me at his betrayal, and I near faint upon witnessing the war club he wields—an eagle's talons clutching a stone ball.

"Whistling Hare," I whisper, knowing a warrior such as he would not part with his club willingly. My thoughts turn to Father, Creek Jumper, and the others in their party. I lean to the side, near retching at the thought of them all slain.

"Rebecca," Sarah says. "What is it?"

My sister's voice calls me back to action. I shove thoughts of Father aside, rising to pull Sarah and Numees to their feet. We three push hard to reach the opening and leave our village behind.

A pair of hooded witches stands beyond the wall, torches lighting their pockmarked and scratched faces. "Mistress," one yells. "They're here!"

I fling my tomahawk to silence her.

The other witch rushes us.

I drop Sarah's arm from my shoulder to meet the witch in the open.

"Go." I say to Numees, positioning myself between them and the witch. "Take my sister from here."

"Rebecca, no," says Sarah.

"Go!"

I keep the witch's focus as my sister and friend stumble away.

"Mistress!" the witch shouts. "They're escaping!"

I maneuver around, circling to reach the dead witch whose skull still holds my tomahawk. I pluck it free, comforted in wielding both weapons.

The witch approaches me. She swings her blade wildly, untrained.

I scream a war cry and rush her, listening to our blades sing together. I catch hers with the edge of mine and shrug it off, then sheathe my long dagger under her chin.

She gasps and chokes as I pull away, thinking to run.

I find my escape barred not only by hooded women but also by native braves.

They fence around me, each of them waving torches to capture my attention as they close in.

I spin around, feinting to keep them at bay.

"Wait," a male voice calls. "Leave her."

To my surprise, they stand off and open their circle for Two Ravens.

"Traitor."

He grins at me. "Did I not say I would gladly make the war dance with you, white girl? Come." He ushers me come near him with Whistling Hare's war club. "Let us dance together now."

I stare in wonder at such a man. Question what defense I can hope to bring against him. Father's teachings remind me speed must be my ally in such a bout. I raise my dagger and tomahawk, moving them in distraction as Two Ravens approaches.

He swings the war club, forcing me back.

The end of it whistles past my face.

I push off my back foot the moment it passes, diving forward before he can swing again. I roll upon the ground, hooking his ankle with the back of my tomahawk, yanking up and slicing him.

He roars at the blow and swings anew.

Again, I duck away and bring my blades to bear.

Horses scream in the distance and riders approach us, each of them yipping and wailing.

I near faint seeing the riders carry Sarah and Numees across their laps.

"Rebecca, run." Sarah shouts. "Go now!"

Madness catches me at the pleading in her voice. I rush Two Ravens, stabbing and hacking. My blades cut him more than once, yet still he stands.

He laughs upon catching my wrist.

I cry out as he twists it back, and I drop my tomahawk.

Two Ravens bashes my nose with the blunt edge of his stolen club.

My world swirls black and red as I drop to my knees. I swing my remaining blade, but even its movement feels slow in my hand.

Two Ravens kicks me in the back, and falls upon me. He presses my face in the dirt and places his knee upon my spine. He first binds my hands tight behind my back then jerks me to my feet.

"Walk," he commands, grabbing my hair and leading me back into the village.

My feet stumble, yet his grasp warns I must not fall.

Burning huts light our way, their animal skins seared away leaving the skeletal remains afire. Dogs who so often chased us through the maze of homes lie dead with arrows in them.

Two Ravens leads me through a maze of bodies, and his braves toss their own dead into the flames with little regard. Some witches stare at me, their eyes hollow. Others pour a blackish-purple powder into their palms then snort it.

We reach the gathering circle, but Two Ravens does not allow me join them. He takes me instead to the striking pole and ties me to it.

My legs collapse, though the leather bindings keep me upright.

Sturdy Oak's old face quivers at the sight of me and his body sags in relent to his bonds.

"I-I am sorry, Grandfather," I say through my tears, "that I could not protect you."

"You speak softly to him?" Two Ravens asks. "Let you speak such sorrow to her, old man. You wrong your women by not fighting."

"He is a peace chief." I spit. "By the law, he cannot fight."

Two Ravens motions his braves lift Sturdy Oak to his feet. Then he looks back at me. "Did your white father not teach you what happens to those who neither fight nor flee, woman?"

"No...don't," I say, watching Two Ravens stroke the ball of his stolen war club against Sturdy Oak's cheek. "Grandfather."

Sturdy Oak looks on me with the same kindness I recall from my youth. "Peace, child," he says. "Do not be troubled."

His calming voices washes over me, even as Two Ravens swings his club.

I wince in the final moment, shutting my eyes to Sturdy Oak's murder, but my ears I cannot close. The *smack* and screams of the people resound in them.

"What's this?" Two Ravens asks, pointing to the prone body of my grandfather. "A sturdy oak felled by Two Ravens?"

The braves and witches join him in laughter.

I stare at their faces, making note of their mirth. Like logs to the flame, they feed my hate.

"Enough," a female voice calls.

I look into the crowd. The hoodless she-devil who killed two of our men approaches, flanked by several witches. She carries a pair of books in hand, and I well recognize the covers of both—my sister's Bible and the Putnam journal.

"Two Ravens," she says. "We must be gone from here before the dawn. Kill the rest, or do with them as you will."

She grins as her eyes fall upon me and then to Sarah.

"Leave me the white squaw and her crippled sister."

The braves carry out her orders, yet Two Ravens remains behind, watching.

"What of those who escaped?" he asks.

"I'll leave behind some of my coven to deal with them," the hoodless woman says. "Pretty voices fare better at singing young birds back to the nest than howling wolves do."

Numees struggles against the men so willfully they knock her unconscious and drag her away by her feet.

I rage against my bonds while others in our village shout obscenities at the raiders for such treatment.

All are greeted with similar brutality.

My spirit near breaks at what I witness, though my mind wonders what power the she-devil holds to keep Two Ravens and his men in her sway as she kneels before me.

I reckon her even older than Father by her wrinkles and the gray in her dirtied hair streaking with the blond. I glare into her face, noting her glittering eyes behind the streak of black painting over them.

"Who are you?" I ask.

"Can it be you do not recognize a devil's daughter, birthed in the evils of Salem?" She holds the Putnam journal aloft. Flips through its pages. "Poor, poor Thomas Putnam." She *tsk*s. "Shall I read you what he wrote of me?"

"Aye," I say. "I would know your name, witch."

"I think that a fair trade," she says. "Being that I know yours, Rebecca Kelly…or should I call you by your *true* family name, Campbell?"

She casts her gaze upon the journal and opens her mouth to read.

"*The sixteenth day of November, sixteen ninety-one. God be praised, and bless Dr. Campbell.*" Her voice rises in a mocking tone. "*A knock came at my door late this eve, and he behind it. My daughter Ann stood with him. So too did my servant, Mercy. "What cause did they have to be out so late at night?" I asked them both. "And alone with a young man too?*"

The woman throws her head back in a fit of laughter that shivers me with its coldness.

"I recall this night well," she says. "Do not let Thomas Putnam fool you with his stern words. He knew well what cause I should have alone with a young man, especially one so handsome as Dr. Simon Campbell. Believe you me, child, my dear

Master Putnam would have had the same of me had I hinted he were welcome to try."

"So you are a whore," I say.

"Among other things." She grins then continues reading Thomas Putnam's journal. "*Dr. Campbell requested to speak with me outside. I consented, but first promised both girls a thrashing upon my return for her disobedience. God help me. My daughter knew my act all for show and exhibited little fear in front of my guest. I shall need to remedy her of that. The child should at least pretend to obey me…as Mercy does.*"

The hoodless woman glances up from the journal, looking from me to Sarah. "And so I kept my pretense for Thomas Putnam. All the many days I spent laboring under his roof. And all the nights until I slew him with my Salem sisters."

"You," Sarah says to her. "You are Mercy Lewis."

"Aye," she answers. "And you are the daughters of Dr. Simon Campbell."

"That man was no father to me," I say.

Mercy laughs. "Fear not, white squaw. I mean you no harm. Dr. Campbell's plot freed me of my burdensome labor in the Putnam house. He revealed to me the invisible world with his Devil's powder. Gifted me and my Salem sisters the means to exact our revenge upon those who looked down on us."

"He was no father to me." I insist.

"I believe that," says Mercy. "A fire rages in you that could not have been learned from Dr. Campbell. His was ever an icy way, cold to the torments his plan wrought upon our village. So tell me, girl, where did you learn such wildness?"

I keep my silence, not wishing to give more away.

"An adopted father, I reckon," says Mercy. "I did the same. And mine would meet you in Boston."

"Cotton Mather..." I say.

Mercy nods.

"Why?" Sarah asks. "Our father died fifteen year ago at the hand of Abigail Williams. Why should anyone care what happened to his children?"

Mercy shrugs. "Let Rebecca ask when we arrive."

She draws a bone-hilted dagger.

The red and black ribbons flutter as I await her to loose my bindings, wondering if it be possible to steal the blade and slay her before the braves kill me.

"The others gave up their search for you lot," Mercy says to me. "Old age and new lives weakened their will. They would have me believe Abigail accomplished the task set before us. That finding Dr. Campbell's body, gutted and strung in the woods, was proof enough vengeance had been served...but I knew some of you yet lived."

Fear wells within me as Mercy stands, turning her attention to Sarah.

"Abigail was always the favorite." Mercy's cheek quivers. "She and her pretty face and still prettier manners. I remember well how she would toy with those she accused and the joy in her face when she watched them dangle on the rope. We shared that delight, she and I. And all the while, I often wondered if she would look so happy at her own death."

The tip of Mercy's blade quivers as she kneels before Sarah.

"Then I heard stories Abigail was slain. Murdered by a daughter of Dr. Campbell." She taps her blade against my sister's shins. "What lames you?"

"God," Sarah says. "He punishes me for my sins."

"No," says Mercy. "He has no place here. These are Satan's lands, filled with heathens."

"God is everywhere," says Sarah.

"Then let Him come down and heal you now," Mercy says. "It is a long march to Boston and the Lord knows I will not be slowed by a cripple."

I struggle against my bonds to no avail as Sarah rises and falls, her legs giving out with each attempt.

"Get up, Sarah," I say. "Stand."

She tries again and fails.

Mercy feigns disappointment. "Will you offer up no prayer?"

"I-it is written," says Sarah. "Thou shalt not tempt the Lord thy God."

My limbs burn with the leather against them when Mercy kicks Sarah's ribs.

"Do you think me a savage who knows naught of the scriptures? That you must quote book and verse to me?" Mercy asks. "I know the good book well, daughter of Campbell. Let you remember Genesis nine and six, 'Whoso sheddeth man's blood, by man shall his blood be shed. For in the image of God made he man."

"Coward whore!" I cry. "Leave my sister be. Let you take me instead."

"And send you to Heaven for your sacrifice? Never." Mercy looks to Two Ravens. "Take the squaw from this place. I will leave a warning for those who would raise their hand against us."

Two Ravens moves too quick for me to react. He palms my forehead, pinching my nose shut and forcing a bit of wood into my mouth ere tying it off behind my head. I scream through it, and feel my bindings loosened as he takes me from the striking pole.

The pain returns an instant later when Two Ravens tightens them so that my blood flow closes off. At his whistle, a brave bring him a horse. He slings me atop its back and binds me to it.

The bit in my mouth muffles my demands as my sister struggles against Mercy, fighting to keep off her back.

But even I know it a one-sided affair as Mercy knocks Sarah in the heads and turn her to her stomach.

"Those who escaped the night Abigail died told me of a girl who fell from the sky," Mercy says, putting her knee in Sarah's back. "Like Lucifer cast down."

The bindings hold me fast despite my struggle.

"P-please," Sarah says through her tears. "Let you take me but leave my sister alone...God save you, leave her be."

"I mean your sister no harm, Sarah Kelly," Mercy says. "But you—"

She takes hold of my sister's hair and yanks Sarah's head back.

"You killed my Salem sister." Mercy brings the edge of her bone dagger to Sarah's forehead. "And I have longed for the chance to repay you in kind."

My teeth near shatter upon the bit at the sound of Sarah's blood-curdling cry. My skin flaming with leather burns as my bonds keep me atop the mount.

My struggle sets the horse to panic. It wheels away from Two Ravens and saves me from witnessing my sister's final moments.

"Enough." Two Ravens yells, reining the horse to calm.

His words mean nothing to me.

My wail rises and an endless flood of tears cascade down

my cheeks as Mercy stands, leaving my sister's lifeless body in the dirt.

Mercy lifts her hand, dyed crimson-black in the firelight.

She holds what I believe a bit of bloodied cloth against the striking pole. Then stabs her bone-hilted dagger, nailing the cloth to the pole. She leaves more than two ribbons fluttering in the wind.

A moment later, I realize it a wrongful claim.

There be only the two ribbons.

The other bits are hair.

My wits leave me at the realization of that which Mercy leaves upon the pole. I taste blood on my tongue, shrieking curses at my sister's killer.

Then Two Ravens appears, striking a blow to my head that sends me into darkness.

-nine-

THE SOUNDS OF THE FOREST WAKEN ME—AN OWL'S HOOT, AND the echo of a wolf pack howling in unison. I look to the sky and note it darker than I remembered. A new night, judging by the moon's placement.

The throbbing in my head speaks I might well have slept the whole of day away. Dizziness bids me fall over, yet my bindings keep me upright and tied to the trunk of an old oak. The taste of dried blood fills my mouth and a raw fire rages in my throat, begging relief.

"Wa…water…" I choke the words.

"Do not look for kind treatment here," says a woman's voice behind me. "You shall receive little and less from this lot."

"Wh-who are you?"

"A captive like you," she says. "And a prized one, for what comfort that may bring me."

"Prized?"

"Aye," she says. "Look you to the west and find those not so prized as we."

Not a few campfires burn from the direction she speaks. The largest of them built some fifty yards away. Laughter and talk hail from some. Moans and cries from others, further off.

"Mercy keeps us separate from your people," the woman behind me says. "She would not risk us fall prey to savage desire for womanly comfort. We at least may be grateful for that."

My soul weeps at the sounds of woe hailing from the direction where my people lay captive. My anger stokes anew at the thought of those who can no longer cry out, my sister chief among them.

"I would show Mercy Lewis how grateful I am," I say, through gritted teeth.

"You would do better to hide your hatred, if you desire your tongue. Mercy will not suffer scorn, if she be anything like the girl I remember from our youth."

"You know her then?" I ask.

"Aye. Much as it pains me," she says. "I know you also, Rebecca Kelly."

I struggle against my bonds to turn and know her better. Instead, I find the bondsman did his work well, and I cannot see for the tree's girth and the surrounding dark.

"Who are you?" I ask.

"We met at your brother's trade post, near one week and a half past. Mary is my name, in the event you forgot, as most are wont to do when meeting me."

I think back and recall the burly trader and his equally large wife's meek demeanor at the table. "I remember you," I say. "Though you were quiet and shy."

"Aye," she says. "It has ever been my way, though I would change it if I could."

Her voice pains me as one who feels deep regret, yet she speaks so blatantly as to make me doubt her words.

"Mary," I say. "If you are here, where is your husband?"

"Dead," she says. "Mercy and her lot happened upon us not a few days past. They killed him before his body knew him murdered. An arrow through his chest without warning."

Mary sighs.

"I should be dead also," she says. "If not for Mercy. All these many years and still she recognized my face."

Mary quiets as a lone torchbearer walks toward us, lighting the brush.

"Murderer," I shout, the moment Mercy steps into my line of sight.

My sister's killer shakes her head. "Peace between us, Rebecca."

"I will never—"

"Then let us have quiet at least," says Mercy.

I scream defiance at her. Fight against my bonds, hoping for a chance to free myself and strangle her.

"You killed my sister." I seethe.

"And she killed mine." Mercy cocks her head to the side. "And so it goes, back to Cain and Abel. Do not judge me harshly, girl. Your father began this game. We three here tonight are but a few of the pieces left upon the board to finish it."

"Aye." I glare at her. "I will finish it."

Mercy laughs at my words. "A kindred spirit is a rare thing. I have lived long enough to recognize that now. We should have been great friends, you and I, if not for this game between our fathers."

I spit at her. "I could never have befriended a murderous whore. I know that is how you keep the natives loyal to you."

Mercy's lip curls, and I relish that my words have stirred such a reaction.

"What could you know of me, girl? Only what Thomas Putnam wrote," Mercy says. "Ah, but I know well of you and yours. Birthed in privilege, then raised among the natives as their own. Taught the freedom in a life among the wild, far from the greed and sway of powerful men. But you have never been made to serve them, not like Abigail and I." She looks past me to the opposite side of the tree. "Nor Mary either."

Her mention of ties confuses me, a sight which must be plain upon my face for Mercy again mocks my ignorance with laughter.

"Did your fellow captive say naught of how she and I know one another? Or would she fill your head with lies, as she is known to do?" Mercy parades around the tree. "Come, Mary. What have you told this poor girl of our kinship?"

"I-I said nothing to her, Mercy," says Mary. "Nothing at all. Only that you recognized me in the woods."

Mercy sneers. "I recognized a traitor."

"Mercy, please—"

"I warned the others you could not be trusted, Mary Warren," says Mercy. "That you would wilt before John Proctor, that old goat you called master. But we, your Salem sisters, set him right. We taught him what happens to men who raise their fists against frightened, pig-faced girls like you. Didn't we, Mary?"

"Aye," says Mary. "And I were glad Proctor hanged with all the rest. Believe me."

"I do not," says Mercy. "Nor will I ever. You near gave us all up when you confessed to a witch. You should be dead already if I were selfish as you. I only allow you live now because it would not serve for me to rob the others of their vengeance."

"Oh, Mercy, please," says Mary. "I could not bear the others. Let you kill me now instead."

"No," says Mercy. "I would rather you think on your sins all the way to Boston. Perhaps your lying tongue will think of more untruths to tell once there, but I shall hear no more of them. And rest assured, Mary Warren, after the others have dealt you their blows and sated their vengeance, it will be me that sees you from this world."

Mercy comes again to my side of the tree. She kneels in front of me and holds a skin of water to my cracked lips.

"Drink," she commands.

I look away.

"You think I mean to poison you?" Mercy drinks deep of the skin. "I should have killed you already, if I wished you dead. Let you drink now."

I look her in the eye. Let her witness my hate plain. "All I would have from you is your life." I glance up at her tangled mess of hair. "And that dirtied pelt upon your head."

Mercy grins at me. "A kindred spirit indeed."

She drinks again of the water skin, smacks her lips with satisfaction.

"We leave at dawn," she says. "Take what rest you can. Tomorrow is a long march."

She leaves me to darkness, her torch wandering toward the campfires. Several times, I attempt to engage Mary, yet my words fall upon deaf ears and she remains a mute to my questions.

Sleep does not come easy. My back and limbs ache with stiffness, and I cannot stretch them despite my efforts. Even when sleep takes me, death haunts my dreams.

I wake before dawn, shivering from the cold. Frost covers the earth, and my breath steams as it leaves my lips. I look out across the forest, noting the campfires burned low.

A lone torch makes its way toward me—Mercy bringing dried strips of venison.

"Eat," she says.

I spurn her attempts to feed me, though my body preaches I must eat soon if I am to keep my strength. The thought of Sarah allows me stave such hunger off.

"Let you starve then," says Mercy.

I say nothing as she feeds my scraps to Mary then leaves us.

"You would do well to heed her," says Mary. "You cannot avenge others if you starve upon the road."

"Is that why you eat?" I ask, my eyes never leaving Mercy's backside. "To avenge your husband?"

"No. I do not mourn the loss of him. He was never good to me," says Mary. "Not that any man has ever been."

"But you married him."

"Aye," she says. "He helped me escape Salem. Sheltered me when others would hunt me down."

"Then he was good to you," I say.

"Fool girl," Mary says. "His protection did not come without cost, I assure you. No man's does."

I think of Father then, though I say naught to Mary of him. She speaks with such conviction that I know my words would be lost on her.

Mercy and Two Ravens return not an hour later, leading a painted mare.

They keep Numees among them. Her face is scratched and dirty, but elsewise unharmed to my eye. My friend maintains her proud spirit, never breaking, despite Two Ravens' rough handling of her.

"We march now," Mercy says to me. "Look you to your friend here. Test me in any way, and I take her pretty hair the same as I did your sister's."

I glance at Numees. The cold in her eyes speaks she would welcome such a fate, rather than again be made a slave to our enemies.

Mercy must sense the same, for she kicks Numees to her knees and brings a knife to my friend's forehead. "Shall I dispense of her now and prove my words?"

"No," I say. "I will follow if you leave her be."

Two Ravens shakes his head. "You disappoint me, girl. I thought you a warrior."

"I am happy to disappoint you," I say, watching Mercy sheathe her dagger and aiding Numees stand.

"Come now, lover." Mercy says to Two Ravens. "Let you not judge her too hastily. Would you not do the same for me?"

He grunts in reply as he approaches me.

I keep my eyes on Numees, a reminder not to flinch or fight as Two Ravens unties me from the tree. He gives me little time to stretch, jerking me up and walking me closer to the horse ere tying me off again.

Mercy stands so near I can smell her breath.

My eyes flit to the knives at her belt.

"Do it." She whispers in my ear. "We have far too many mouths to feed. I should gladly rid myself of one more."

I look her in the eye.

"Or perhaps I need not kill her quickly," says Mercy. "Mayhap I should only take her eye to remind you. Or would you prefer her ear instead? Learn you to listen?"

I glance away to the tune of Mercy's laughter and stare at the tree line to calm myself.

Two Ravens reappears, hauling Mary Warren. She stumbles next to me, barely catching herself, as our captor ties her to the same mount. He takes Numees next, his hand grabbing her roughly by the arm.

My friend says nothing as he leads her away, nor does she bother look on me.

I know not how to feel of what Numees might wish of me. Whether she truly desired me oppose Mercy and have her killed for it, or if she, too, is numb to our predicament. I have little time to ponder, as Mercy swings astride the mare.

"Let us be gone from here."

She kicks the mare's ribs. The rope between my hands grows taut and tugs me to walk behind it. As if to prove her point, Mercy leads us through the camp forcing me witness the faces of those who yet live from my village.

They too are bound, though not behind any mount. Leather thongs tie their hands and necks to branches that keep them in line with one another.

A few struggle to stand, and the collective suffer for it. My heart goes out to them, though some of the younger ones look on me with disdain at the special treatment Mary and I receive.

I hang my head that they might know I suffer with them, in spirit if not in body.

All day we march northeastward. I stare at the back of Mercy's head, all the while imagining myself taking her scalp living as she took Sarah's. The lone thought keeps me going. Step after step, even when thirst and hunger bid me fall.

By nightfall, I find even vengeful thoughts tiresome.

I collapse beside the tree Two Ravens leads me to, thankful to sit and rest. He gives me his skin of water. I guzzle it down and near retch for drinking it too quick.

Again, he ties Mary opposite me before abandoning us.

I gather she and I will not speak much this night, to judge by her labored breathing. Despite it all, I think her stronger than first I credited, for I, too, am wearisome and younger than half her age, if I judge her rightly.

Sleep finds me easier, plunging me into more nightmares. This night, I dream again on my *manitous*. Unlike the vision in my dream fast, I am tied to a tree. Forced to endure witnessing the raccoon slip behind me, and feel its sharpened teeth nibbling at my wrists.

I wake to Mary's snores and find the biting pain still pinches me.

Something tugs at my bonds.

I struggle against it. Hoping to scare the animal off.

A gentle hand touches my shoulder. Squeezes.

I turn my head, and gasp at the painted war face that appears beside me.

"Father..."

-ten-

FATHER RAISES A SINGLE FINGER TO HIS LIPS, USHERING ME SILENT.

I lean back to the tree, listening to the scratching sound of his blade upon the bonds holding me. The constriction around my wrists loosens, bit by bit, until the last of them breaks. My arms fall limp at the sudden freedom.

Father places his guiding hand beneath my arm and helps me stand.

Tears sting my face as I throw my arms around him. My body heaves as I pull him close and feel his strength wash over me when he returns my embrace. I struggle to keep him near when he releases his hold and pulls away. He looks me in the eye with a tenderness that tells me I need not speak of Sarah's fate.

My mind floods with questions at the sight of him injured also. Deep cuts line his body and one wound upon his chest yet bears a broken arrow shaft.

He uses his hands to speak with me, motioning we must be off southward.

I look over my shoulder toward the campfires, my thoughts going out to Numees.

Father shakes his head when I glance at him.

In my heart, I know him right. We two cannot risk rescuing all our people, especially not with he injured and me worn from travel. The thought of leaving her to torment and slavery tears at me though and keeps me from leaving.

Dried leaves rustle by the tree, and Mary snorts awake.

"Wh-who's there?" She asks.

Father pulls at my arm and jerks his head that we should leave.

"Rebecca?" Mary asks. "Is that you?"

She struggles against her bonds.

"*Rebecca,*" she hisses. "Speak to me, girl."

Father wastes no time in yanking me away.

"Don't leave me," she near yells. "Rebecca. Please, come back!"

Father leads me into the forest. We leap over fallen logs and sprint through brushes that tear at my skin.

Men shout behind us and horses whinny.

"Rebecca!" Mary calls.

I glance back, spying lit torches and hearing new voices.

Both gift my legs new strength.

Father stops of a sudden, and I near tumble beside him. He motions for me to head right, then pushes me off.

My pulse quickens when he goes the opposite direction, knocking his blades against the trees. Running over dried leaves. Making his presence known to all creatures of the forest.

I chance another look over my shoulder and witness the torches veer in Father's direction. A few continue on toward me.

Father howls a war cry, and the few meandering torches right themselves toward him.

I hesitate to move onward. My thoughts torn between what Father would have me do and the thought of losing him.

The sounds of scuffling fill the air—blades clashing, and the screams of those in death's throes.

I wheel about, running in the direction of the torches, then skulking in the shadows as I near the battle. I find Father encircled by not a few braves.

Several others lie twitching near him.

Blood flows from Father's open wounds, yet still he fends them off, making each pay with their lives for any misstep.

A brave passes near me without noticing my presence. He lifts his flintlock, taking aim at Father.

I grab a nearby rock and leap from my position and dash his head in. I waste little time in stealing his knives, then take up his rifle also. I swing its aim to bear. Smoke fills the air before me as I shoot dead a hooded witch come up behind Father. I drop the rifle and leave off, knowing the smoke gives away my position.

I keep to the shadows, sneaking upon any who chance my path, taking two more braves in the same manner before the scuffling halts.

I look to Father and see he yet stands, the braves and witches backing off him.

Then I understand why.

Swinging Whistling Hare's club in practice, Two Ravens steps toward Father.

Jeers rise from those around them as both men square off.

Helplessness pangs my gut at learning us far outnumbered. Though the many are distracted, my conscience warns I might take only one or two before the others make an end of me.

Instead, I am forced to watch as Father and Two Ravens battle.

Several times, I think the larger warrior's swing will be the end of Father, yet always its stone edge catches naught but air. And for every swing Two Ravens makes, a new wound is made upon his body.

Father's tomahawk and long knife dance in such a way to distract the eye of any who watch. Twice he makes Two Ravens pay for biting at his feints.

My hopes rise, witnessing the anger plain in Two Ravens face. He again mistakes his strength for victory when he brings his club down in a swinging arc.

Father catches it between his blades, twisting the club from his enemy's grasp, then knocking his head against Two Ravens.

The rival champion stumbles back, and I near shout when Father hooks his ankle, tripping him up. With a feral cry, Father raises his tomahawk high to end Two Ravens.

Someone yanks my hair back and presses a cold blade's edge upon my throat.

"Alden!"

The shout in my ear near deafens me, but Father stays his hand. Turns to learn who called him by his true surname, his face awash with anger. Upon the sight of me held captive, he tosses both his weapons aside with little regard.

"Walk," Mercy whispers, then guides me closer to Father.

Two Ravens climbs to his feet. He picks up the war club and raises it to cave in Father's head.

"Wait." Mercy bids him. "His life is worth more than all the captives you have."

Two Ravens lowers the club. "Why?"

"You know him as Black Pilgrim," says Mercy. "And I once called him Priest. Only later did I learn his truth. His father were an Alden, and his family has long plagued my adopted father. Let him live now and profit from the bounty on his head."

Her words and voice strike an odd chord in me. She speaks in such a way that lends me to believe she knows Father well.

Two Ravens kicks Father in the back, knocking him into the dirt.

"Bind him," he commands his braves.

"Stop!" I cry.

"Aye," says Mercy. "Do not harm him."

The braves do not listen. Each falls upon Father like vultures on a carcass.

Despite it all, he endures their rough treatment wordlessly.

"I said leave him be," says Mercy, shoving me into the arms of a hooded witch and slinking toward Father.

Two Ravens meets her in the middle. "We take no more orders from you, woman."

"You defy me?" she asks.

"I have always defied you," he says. "But in silence until this night. He is my prisoner."

"You should be dead if not for me," Mercy hisses. "He stopped only when hearing me call his name."

"Then you should not have named him," says Two Ravens. "And he would belong to you still. It was Two Ravens who fought him. He belongs to me."

Mercy looks on Father and chews her lip.

"Let you name your price then," says Mercy. "And my father will pay it when I arrive in Boston."

"Your money and father mean little to me," says Two Ravens. "The white slavers will pay me enough for our captives. As for Black Pilgrim, I will gift him to our newest nation in friendship."

"You would give him to the Tuscarora?" Mercy asks.

"I will," says Two Ravens. "Their hatred yet burns great for that night long ago when he killed their people and your witches. And I hear others are angry with me for raiding without their leave." He points to Father with the war club. "His blood will heal the wounds of all and earn me honor for his capture."

Mercy draws close to Two Ravens, her finger grazing across his chest.

"Perhaps we can make a trade," she says.

Two Ravens laughs. "You have nothing left to offer, witch. I have no wont for your Devil's powder and my braves have little need of your women now that we have captives. As for your offer"—he bats her hand away—"what man desires more of the soured fruit he has already tasted?"

Mercy shrieks and swings her blade.

Two Ravens catches her by the wrist.

Mercy's witches hurry to her aid then retreat when Two Ravens' braves step toward them.

He looks to his men. "Get him up and ready the others. We leave now. I'll not wait for this murderous witch to kill me in my sleep."

Mercy rises, her gaze flitting between Father and Two Ravens, his braves and her witches.

"Let me speak with him," Mercy says, her voice pleading. "Please."

Two Ravens glares at her. "You think me a fool? That I should let you kill him before my eyes?"

I pull back when Mercy throws her weapons aside, and I witness the same confusion in Two Ravens.

"Why should you wish to speak with him?" he asks.

"Because," her voice flutters, "I would speak with my husband one final time."

My mind reels at her words, warns she misspoke.

"Husband?" Two Ravens asks.

"Aye," says Mercy. "Though he left me long ago...and with child."

I look on Father, expecting him to rage at such blatant lies, but when he meets my eyes there be no denial in them. No anger. Only shame.

Two Ravens steps aside, motioning Mercy over to Father.

Tears well in my eyes as she kneels beside him, brushes matted and bloodied hair from his brow.

"F-forgive me," says Mercy to Father. "I had not thought it should ever come to this."

Father says nothing in reply, yet he does not look away.

"I have missed you so, Priest," says Mercy. "You were ever the only man to keep my affection. Will you speak now? Tell me why it is you left me with child, never for me to see you again until this day?"

I wish he would denounce her claims, name her liar and spit on Sarah's killer.

He gives only silence.

"I knew you for a rogue when first I took you into my arms," she says. "And hate has long burned in my heart from your leaving. Yet as I look on you now, I know that I should make the mistake again for the child you gave me. Will you not ask about h—"

"No," says Father, his voice gruff and low.

Mercy sits on her heels, rage crossing her face. She grabs hold of the arrow shaft in Father's chest. His face reddens and he winces as she plucks it free, yet he utters no word, no cry of pain as Mercy flings the shaft away.

It lands in the brush near me.

The hooded witch beside me pays it little mind, her attention on her mistress and my father.

My gaze warily turns to the bloodied arrowhead, and I know it within my reach if only the witch remains distracted.

"I have thought long on what I should do or say if ever I met you again," Mercy says to Father. "And for all my hate…all my fury…in the end, I thought only of this."

Mercy takes my father's whiskered cheeks in her hands. She leans to him, kissing his lips, holding him in the moment.

Father does not return her affections.

The hooded witch beside me crows at the sight of her mistress kissing Father.

I use the moment to scoot nearer the arrowhead, and notice Father sees me.

When Mercy pulls away, he leans forward of a sudden, kissing her fully.

Again, those around me cheer at the sight.

I reach the broken arrow shaft. I find myself able to palm and snap off the arrowhead, and tuck it inside my belt ere Mercy pulls away from Father.

"Goodbye, Priest," she says. "For now and always."

She leaves his side and takes up his dagger from the dirt, the one gifted him by his own father.

"I will give this to our child," she says, sheathing it in her belt. "A lone gift from a bastard father."

I meet Father's gaze, my eyes pleading him renounce her claims, or speak one soft word to me.

He will not. Even as the braves haul him away, he passes on his willful defiance for his captors to me.

Even then, I cannot form the words as to what I should speak to him.

In the end, he only nods before the braves force him away, disappearing into the forest.

"You will truly leave me here then?" Mercy asks Two Ravens.

"You have your witches," he says. "And your two prisoners. Is that not what you came for?"

"A company of women." Mercy jeers. "We shall be taken upon our first steps into Iroquois lands and burned alive, no doubt. I wonder—" She saunters toward him. "Would you have me speak ill of you when that occurs?"

Confusion crosses the face of Two Ravens.

"Should I tell the Six Nations all you have done without their approval?" she asks. "Or will you grant me an envoy and safe passage through Iroquois lands, that I might tell them of your greatness? Whisper in my English father's ear of how Two Ravens and his people are truly friends to us and ours?"

Two Ravens grins. "Or perhaps I kill you now."

"Aye," she says. "You could indeed. But you know well the reach of my English father. Kill me at your peril."

"Has no one told you how I came by my name, woman?" He asks. "Two Ravens cares nothing for white men. French or English, he bends them to his will and pits them against one another, killing two ravens with one stone. In the end, the Iroquois stay strong."

"For now," says Mercy. "But the Iroquois remain so because they are also wise. Let you be wise now, Two Ravens. Grant my request. Give us safe passage and let you make friends on all sides."

I witness the debate in his eyes, his gaze studious of Mercy.

"I will leave you two of my men," he says finally. "Let you sing my praises, little bird. All the way through my people's lands and then into your English father's ear. For if you don't"—he looms over her—"you will learn how far my own reach extends. Even into your colonies."

Mercy grins at his answer. She spins away from him and hauls me to my feet.

I honor my father's silence, saying nothing as she guides me back toward the camp. As her hooded vanguard flanks us for the march, I take careful note of their number, counting fewer than ten since our skirmish.

Two Ravens and his men have readied the captives from my village by the time we arrive. They wail at seeing Father among them. His body bloodied and beaten, eyes and cheeks already swelling with bruises.

He lends his courage to them, keeping his silence whilst Two Ravens and his braves knock him with blows until he falls unconscious beneath their strikes.

It takes all my strength not to cry out for him. I refuse to look away, searing the memory of him handled so poorly in my mind that I might use it to feed my fire.

My people also honor him, even when the braves rally them over to witness their fallen war chief. They force our people to watch Two Ravens disgrace Father further.

He binds one end of rope round Father's ankles, ties the other end off around a stallion's neck. Then he swings astride the beast, gives a war cry, and kicks its ribs.

The stallion jerks forward, and I witness Father's head bounce upon the earth as it drags him away.

I keep my stare of Father until he vanishes from sight. My gut retches from his loss, but my stomach has little to give over. I glance up, all my strength gone, as the braves march my people away.

I keep my stare until long after they are gone and Mercy has tied me to the tree again.

My hatred burns even as the fire embers diminish and the cold of night embraces me. The snores of the hooded guard Mercy set to keep watch signal me to action.

I scoot my back against the tree, feel the arrowhead press into my back. My fingers pluck it free. The sharp and slick-coated edges cut my skin, twining my blood with Father's.

I fix the image of him in my mind.

Think on Sturdy Oak and our people.

Remember Sarah and her sacrifice.

Holding the arrowhead between my thumb and forefinger, I rub its edge against the leather thongs binding me to the tree.

My gaze homed on Mercy.

-eleven-

My wrists and fingers ache as I whittle at the last of the bonds. The sky lightens with each passing moment, its hue violet with the approaching dawn. I work furiously at the bindings, knowing Mercy and the others will waken with the morning sun.

The last of the bindings falls.

I flex my fingers wide and scurry to my feet.

The guard snores as I slip toward her. My thoughts drift to Father and all he taught me of honor as I kneel beside the witch, slipping the dagger at her waist from its sheath.

I stare on her face, pockmarked and scratched, picked at. She can be no older than I, yet her body seems more withered and worn. I wonder if she were one that cackled in my village, and I picture her laughing while my sister screamed.

Then I forget myself.

I cup my hand over the witch's mouth and slide the dagger across her throat, granting her a merciful, quiet death that her mistress robbed from Sarah.

The witch's eyes flutter open as her spirit leaves, the morning cold making it visible as it rises into the morning sky.

I change my attention to the remaining guards. I count their number at near twenty, including Mercy.

The sun peeks beyond the horizon, warning I must hurry.

Murmuring behind me, Mary stirs in her sleep.

I make my way toward her with the witch's dagger in hand.

Mary's head rocks from side to side, tortured in a dream, or so I suppose.

The memory of her waking the guards takes hold of me. I kneel beside her, look on the freshly blooded dagger, then to Mercy and her followers who yet sleep.

My mind hurries me.

I cup my hand over Mary's mouth.

Her eyes widen as I raise the blade to my lips, ushering her quiet before cutting her loose.

Tears well in her eyes as she brings her wrists away from the tree and rubs life into them.

I point to the dead witch then drag my thumb across my throat in silent play at what needs be done.

Darkness crosses Mary's face upon my helping her stand. She hugs me close once finding her feet.

I pull away, see her face beset with grimness.

Mary takes the dagger from my hand, surprising me with her quick and silent way. She moves about the witches, falling upon each as if she plucked the heads off chickens.

I too move among our captors, fetching up a new blade. I gift them the long sleep and think on my loved ones as each death brings me closer to taking the one I crave most.

Indeed, it seems to me that Mary and I race through Mercy's guards, each of us hoping to reach her first.

But I am younger and faster than she, more determined.

I stalk to Mercy, my thoughts on Sarah as I kneel beside her killer.

Reaching for Mercy's hair, a familiar titter calls in the trees above me.

I glance up.

A raccoon nestles in the crook of a branch, watching me from behind its natural black mask, its head cocked to the side.

Creek Jumper's words rise in my mind.

I feel no fear now. Only hate.

A war cry screams behind me—Mary struggling against one of the braves Two Ravens gave over to Mercy.

The other brave stands beside them, his face plain in confusion as he looks upon the camp and sees the witches slain.

Our gazes meet and he wastes no time in leaving, springing into the woods.

Then I am knocked aside with a blow beneath my chin.

My head rocks back, and I stumble away to see Mercy rise from her slumber with murder in her eyes.

"Rebecca," Mary shouts. "Help!"

The brave sits atop her, holding her fist, forcing the dagger toward her.

I throw my blade without thinking and see it buried in his throat even as something cuts my own flesh. The pain draws my attention back to Mercy.

"A kindred spirit indeed," she says. "We truly ought to have been great friends, Rebecca Kelly."

She wields my Father's dagger before me, taunting me come near.

The sight of my own blood staining its blade fills me with rage. I scream and rush Mercy, not caring if she slices me again as I reach for her face.

The blade scratches across my back.

Mercy cries out as I yank her hair.

I sweep my foot behind hers, felling Mercy to earth with

me upon her. My vision floods red and Sarah's face rises in my mind as I dash Mercy's head against the ground, pounding it over and over until she releases the dagger.

"Rebecca..." Mary says behind me.

I fetch the dagger up and raise it over my head.

Mercy looks on me, her nose broke, face bloodied and scratched. "Do it," she spits.

The blade's hilt feels slippery in my hand. I grit my teeth and tighten my grasp upon it.

"Rebecca," says Mary. "He's escaping."

I keep my focus on Mercy. My hatred burning, begging my hand fall and take vengeance for my sister.

"Do it and die," Mercy says. "Or keep me and learn what I know."

The raccoon titters above me, its voice calling the red sight from me. I look to the trees and spy my *manitous* looking down on me.

"What could you know?" I ask Mercy.

She grins at me, despite the blood staining her teeth. "Did you not wonder how your entire war party fell before us?"

"Your traitorous dog drew them out," I say.

"Aye, Two Ravens deceived your people, but we could not have defeated him so soundly without greater numbers." Mercy grins. "There be more of my kind, girl. A second party, headed north even as we speak."

"Why north?" I ask.

"It be a five day trek by land from your village to your brother's trading post, no?"

Fear clutches me at Mercy's words.

"What was his name again," she continues. "George?"

"No..."

Mercy chuckles. "George and his wife, Hannah. And Andrew Martin also." Her lip curls. "Them and the old man."

The blade quivers in my hands.

"Would you know more from me, Rebecca?" Mercy asks. "Make your decision and soon. Two Ravens cannot have gone far yet. No doubt fear hastens the savage your lady servant allowed escape."

I glance back at Mary, see her wringing her hands and her face beset.

"Two Ravens will not return for you," I say to Mercy.

"Not for me," she says. "But the brave you slew, that one over there." Mercy motions to the corpse with a dagger in his throat. "That was his brother, left behind to keep watch over me and ensure I sang loud my song of praise throughout the land."

"Liar," I say.

Mercy sneers. "I am many things, girl, but a liar is not one of them. Look to the one behind you if desiring to know the face of betrayal."

"Rebecca," says Mary. "Don't listen to her. She will say anything to keep her life."

"Ha," cries Mercy. "Let you ask Mary Warren which among us in Salem betrayed her sisters."

I look to Mary.

"No," she says. "It's not true."

"She abandoned us when the tides did not suit her," Mercy coos.

"I came back, Mercy!" Mary says. "Why can you and the others not remember that?"

The pleading in Mary's voice makes me think otherwise. I cannot bring myself to silence Mercy, desiring more knowledge of both women in my company.

"She wilted before her master, John Proctor. Just as she wilted last evening and could not kill the brother of Two Ravens today." Mercy looks on me. "Was it not her shouts that led to your and Priest's capture, Rebecca? You and he would be far from here if not for her weakness."

Her words ring true in my mind, and my gaze wavers between the two while I discern which Salem sister speaks truer.

"Please, Rebecca." Mary trembles. "She is a liar. You must believe me."

"I know not what to believe," I say.

"Then hear my words," says Mercy. "Two Ravens will not suffer you when he learns his kin slain by your hand. Let you take me now to your brother's post that we might warn him. Should Two Ravens fall upon us before we reach it, give me a blade and I will stand beside you."

I scoff. "I am no fool to give you a weapon."

"Only a fool would say so," says Mercy. "The wisest accept they cannot know all. Have you not heard me say I mean you no harm? Let us be frank now—I have no love for the savages. All that I do is to carry out my father's plans."

"What plans?" I ask.

Mercy grins. "Kill me here and you shall never know."

"Do not be misled, Rebecca," says Mary. "Her conniving tongue will bewitch you and earn your trust. Then she will slip a knife in your back as she did to me in Salem."

"And Mary will abandon you at the first hint of trouble," says Mercy. "As she has proven time and again."

I hesitate on what to do. My anger wishes me slay Mercy and be done with it, my mind curious as to the truths she sows among the lies, if any.

"How do I know my brother still lives?" I ask Mercy. "Your dog drew my people out once. Who is to say you do not lead me into another trap?"

"Perhaps I do, but he will die if you judge me wrongly and us with him," says Mercy. "You doubt me and I cannot fault you for it, so let me speak more honestly that you might heed my words."

"There be no means for me know you speak truth."

"Oh, but there is," says Mercy. "You think of me as whore to the natives, Rebecca, and you are right I allowed them love me for a time, but let your cowardly friend speak now on the reason I came to live in Salem."

Her gaze shifts over my shoulder.

"What brought me to serve in the Putnam house, Mary Warren?" says Mercy.

Mary shakes her head. "Do not let her sway you, Rebecca. I beg you."

"Go on," says Mercy. "Speak plain of what befell my goodly family at the hands of the Wabanaki. Tell Rebecca how they were torn limb from limb and roasted over their fires whilst cowardly men of God like that cursed Reverend George Burroughs escaped the Devil's minions."

Her words fright me for what Father may endure at the hands of Two Ravens.

"Aye," says Mary. "And still you serve the savages after that? Your actions alone speak to your treacherous ways."

"You could not fathom my sacrifices, turncoat," says Mercy.

"Long reaching plans were set in motion before the trials in Salem began. We favored few were chosen to move the game along. Do you think I should let a savage even look upon me were it not for the greater good?" Mercy spits. "I pity your short-sighted ways, Mary Warren."

Mercy's venom for Mary catches me as one of a deep, underlying hate, a kind to mirror my own and one derived from truth.

"What is this greater good you speak of?" I ask her.

Mercy grins. "Take me to George's post, and I will speak of what I know."

"Kill her, Rebecca," says Mary. "Kill her now and be done with it."

I discount Mary's skittish voice, instead keeping my watch on Mercy.

"Why do you care so much of my brother's post?" I ask.

"I wish to live," she says. "And we three here are not enough to withstand Two Ravens alone in the woods. It might be your brother and Andrew Martin could help us turn the tide, along with their defenses."

"Two Raven is your friend," I say.

"Then you are a fool," says Mercy. "He will kill me the same as you when learning his brother died among my company. Faulting me for the action, no doubt. Now let us be off, and quickly. We may move faster than he, burdened with his captives, but he will not rest at the news of his slain brother."

The raccoon above me titters anew.

I look on its face, then to my captive's. Creek Jumper warned of overcoming fear, yet Mercy does not fright me. Instead, I find myself drawn to the painted line of black across her eyes, mimicking the raccoon's, and I wonder what my *manitous* would have me learn from her.

The raccoon chatters at me again then leaps from one branch to the next, journeying westward, bound in the direction of my brother's trade post.

I pull Mercy to her feet and take my father's dagger from her. Sticking the point to her back, I urge her toward the tree she tied me to.

"Mary," I say. "Gather up those scraps and tie her hands with them. She's coming with us."

"You make a grievous error," says Mary, even as she carries out my orders.

"Aye, she does," says Mercy, looking to me. "You and I are woodland creatures, Rebecca, swift and free. We should move all the faster without a farm animal to burden us."

"You are coming with me," I say to Mercy. "Mary may go or come as she wishes."

The larger woman's body quivers at my suggestion.

"Then come with us," I say to Mary. "But you must keep up and stay silent."

Mercy laughs. "Can a sow move quietly through the woods?"

"Aye." I glare at her. "That is how your witch sisters came to meet their end."

Mercy's eyes glaze over the dead witches with little regard.

"These here were no true sisters to me," she says. "Only addicts and dregs. You would do well to take their scalps before we leave."

I look on her with horror for the easy tone with which she speaks of her followers.

"Aye," Mercy continues. "Carry them to Boston and pass

their hair off as once belonging to the heathens. The bounty on savage heads was near three pounds per scalp when last I left."

Mary's hand draws across her face.

"Gather what food and water they kept on them," I say to her. "Leave them their hair. We are not savages."

"Not yet," says Mercy.

"Move." I shove her forward.

We are not long on our journey before I learn Mercy spoke one truth at least—Mary both slows us and does not move quietly.

Still, I cannot bring myself to leave her behind.

All day we push on, me driving Mercy ahead and Mary struggling to keep up.

We speak little, though my mind races with inquiries I would ask the two Salem accusers. I make notes of each in my mind, thinking to question both Mercy and Mary once I have them alone.

We continue on well after dusk, me gazing skyward all the while to follow the stars and guide our course. Only when the moon shines directly over us and Mary collapses do we stop for the night.

"I shall take the first watch," I tell her. "Let you sleep for now."

Mary scarcely acknowledges me before bedding down. Her snores ring in my ears before even I finish binding Mercy to a tree.

"We should keep moving," Mercy says. "She will never know we've gone until the morrow. And she could not hope to track or catch us."

I look on Mary's backside. Remembering her earlier fright, I remind myself I, too, was once afraid of the woods and the secrets they held before Father taught me truth.

"We're not leaving her," I say.

"Do you value her more than the lives of your family?" Mercy asks.

"I valued my sister, Sarah," I reply.

"No," says Mercy. "You pitied her."

I backhand her across the mouth. "Do not speak of my sister."

Mercy works her jaw back and forth, but she keeps her quiet as I take a seat well enough away from her.

"Now," I say. "You promised me truths. What do you know of my father?"

"The infamous Dr. Simon Campbell?"

"No, I care nothing for that man." I say. "I would learn more of Priest."

"I should think you know better of him than I," she says.

"You named him husband."

"Ah." Mercy chuckles. "Aye. We were married once, though, in truth, few might name it that. Say instead we gave ourselves to each other, joined as one under the Mother Moon in the sight of my Salem sisters."

"No," I say. "He is a goodly man and loyal."

"Aye. I thought him so too once," says Mercy. "Every man is until he leaves you, dear."

I sneer. "Mary spoke true. You are a liar."

"Believe what you will. I neither care nor worry any longer on what other women think of me. Name it a lone gift of aging." Her voice drops. "But let you remember, Priest did not deny my claim."

I hang my head at that. Keep my quiet.

"Did you note the way he kissed me at the last?" Mercy asks, after a time. "Many a night I thought to skewer him if ever again I saw his face. And yet when my time came...I desired but one more salute from his lips."

"He only did so that I might gain freedom from you," I say, relishing that I might ruin her memory. "The arrowhead you plucked from his chest granted me that."

"Is that so?" Mercy asks. "Sacrificed to free you, eh?"

"Aye."

Mercy chuckles. "God save me, but it were worth it."

I wish she would say more of their relationship, but Mercy will not reveal it. Instead, she sits with her back at the tree, staring at me as if she might read my thoughts.

"More and more I understand why he favors you," she says.

"Do you?"

"Aye. I think we should have been a wonderful family in another life," says Mercy. "The three of us wild and ruthless. Instead, we find ourselves enemies."

I flex my grip upon the dagger's hilt. "I never named you so until you slew my sister."

"Speak not of me so evilly," says Mercy. "We both know I freed her."

I rise and pace toward her.

"Will you strike me for words alone?" she asks. "Or that they strike an equal chord within you?"

"My sister—"

"Was already dead when I came to your village," says Mercy.

I think on Sarah in our hut, how she asked who would be the one to free her of her pain and the suggestion I might end it for her.

"No," I say.

"Come," says Mercy. "Which of us now is the truth-teller and which the deceiver?"

"You did not know her," I seethe.

"I did not need to. The things one keeps speaks all you ever need know of a person, girl," says Mercy. "Tell me, why do you not wear such an elegant dress as she? Silk and lace, pretty things for a pretty girl."

"What do such things matter?"

"Nothing of their own standing," says Mercy. "Had you met me in Boston, you would have seen me dressed the same as your sister."

I near laugh picturing Mercy in such a dress, the thought of the witch passing herself off as a lady striking me odd.

"You are a traitor to yourself then," I say. "If you pretend at two people when in different company."

"Call me a survivor," says Mercy. "An orphaned girl with no prospects and no family must learn to wear the masks others would have of her. And so I did, wearing one for Putnam, another for Dr. Campbell, even this wild mask for Two Ravens and his men."

"Then Mary spoke true," I say. "You are a liar. A deceiver of men."

"Let you not judge me too harshly," says Mercy. "You who also wear a mask to please men."

"No," I say. "I am what you see."

"You came to live with the natives as a young girl, but you were not born among them," says Mercy. "Fifteen years in the wilderness and yet your sister and brother, aye, and Andrew Martin too, remain true to their roots. You alone took on the native ways. Why?"

My blood warms at her words, though I do not quiet her.

"To please Priest," she says. "Not that I may fault you for that. I should have worn any mask he asked of me when he and I first met. Odd, isn't it? He was the only man to never ask me don a disguise."

She pauses, allowing me feel her struggle. I wrestle with such emotions as to pity her, and pull the memory of Sarah to mind, warding off such sentiments, reminding myself to take Mercy's words with a grain of salt.

"Think what you will of me," she says. "Those who cling to the past have no future. I will go to my grave insisting I freed your sister of her pain."

I rise again, my knuckles white upon the hilt of Father's dagger. I hold the blade's edge before Mercy's eyes that she might recognize the Alden family name inscribed upon it.

"Then let you go to your grave with this knowledge also," I say. "Your freedom from pain will come neither easy, nor quick, but it will be at my hand and with my father's dagger."

"A kindred spirit indeed," says Mercy. "Let you remember I named you as such should the time ever come."

"You think I should wilt?"

"I think you are more like me than you realize," says Mercy. "It is why you yet live, that and vengeance."

"Aye, vengeance only."

"A noble thing, that," says Mercy. "I sowed its seed deep within me when the Wabanaki slew my family and watered it with the blood of those who wronged me in Salem."

"And my sister," I say. "How did Sarah wrong you?"

Mercy's cheek quivers. "She stole a life that was mine to take."

"In that she married Priest?" I humph.

"No," says Mercy. "When she killed Abigail Williams."

My brow furrows. "But you were Salem sisters."

"Sisters quarrel," says Mercy.

I say no more, remembering mine own disagreement with Sarah, though I think nothing should have placed a murderous desire in my heart for her.

"What did she do to earn such scorn from you?" I ask. "Abigail?"

"Much and more that matters little now," says Mercy. "The worms feasted on her long ago, as with most of the others from that cursed Salem Village. No doubt, they all wait for me in Hell to wage our war for all eternity. All reasons I would rather dwell here a little longer."

"You shall join her soon, I promise you," I say.

"I've heard many promises in my life," says Mercy. "Few have come to pass." She rests her head against the tree trunk. "Would you have more answers from me, white squaw? Or may I sleep now?"

I leave her side. "Take what rest you can. I shall be here when you wake."

She shuffles against her bonds, settling in for the night.

I yawn upon listening to her soft breathing minutes later, and feel my own eyes heavy with similar fatigue.

The cold of night aids me in my watch for a while. Not two hours later, my body calls me to sleep, willing my eyelids closed. I slap myself awake, convincing myself that Mercy might play asleep though her body has not stirred since last she spoke.

My mind warns to wake Mary, let her take a watch.

The next I know, I open my eyes to the morning dawn.

I bolt upright, and find Mercy, yet tied to the tree, watching me with her green eyes.

"Lovely morning," she says. "Did I wake you?"

Forgetting her taunt, I look behind me to find Mary still sleeps, her body like grizzly lain upon the ground.

I poke her awake.

Mary groans as she rolls over. She yawns wide and scratches herself before sitting up, leaves and moss in her hair. She looks around, rubs sleep from her eyes. "Why did you not wake me for a watch?"

"I—"

The sound of horses ushers me silent. Their hooves crunch the underbrush so loud I know it must be a white man. A native war party would not be so foolish as to lead the beasts through the wood in hopes of surprise.

Mary's eyes widen in fright.

"*Free me,*" Mercy hisses. "Do it now and give me a blade. Let me stand beside you."

I shake my head no when Mary looks for my answer.

"Stay here," I say. "Keep her quiet."

I gather up my things. Slipping into the forest shadows, silent as a fox, I pad closer to the noise and crouch behind a fallen tree. My left hand gravitates to the hilt of Father's long knife, clasps it for comfort as I lie in wait.

The party crosses into my line of sight, though the monstrous lead stallion blocks my vision of the person who leads it.

A lesser horse marches behind the first, the two tethered together. This one carries blankets and clothes—dyed shirts, stockings, and bolts of wool cloth. Frayed edges of rope signal me the owner cut their ends. I understand why when seeing the third and final horse, a white mare.

Blood streaks down its pale skin, all from an elder brave, slung across her back and the rope bindings that tie him there.

As the train passes me by, I look on the face of the unconscious Indian brave and gasp.

"Creek Jumper..."

-twelve-

THE HORSES NEIGH AS I MAKE MY PRESENCE KNOWN.

With Father's dagger drawn, I swing around the white mare to learn who carries our shaman bundled to the horse.

I near drop the dagger when seeing who leads the train—a boy on the eve of manhood. His face painted for war, though he appears more as one who would play at war than fight in one.

"Rebecca..." Ciquenackqua drops the reins. He stumbles toward me and falls into my arms, his body heaving.

I hug him tight, pressing his head against my shoulder.

"I thought you dead." I pull away to look on his face, ensure he is real and not a vision sent to torture me.

"I-I should be," he says. "I should have stayed and fought with the others."

"What happened?"

"D-dead," he cries. "All of them killed by Two Ravens and his men. White women fought also. They surprised us on the riverbank as our men slept."

I shudder at the thought, near retching at them caught off guard.

"Two Ravens," says Ciquenackqua. "H-he killed my father and took his war club. I-I could not save him."

"I know. He carried it when they raided our village."

"Did you see my mother?" he asks. "Is she with you?"

"She were taken." I hang my head at Ciquenackqua's wails. "Along with all the rest who survived the attack."

I pat Ciquenackqua's back, soothe him the best I know how.

"Listen to me now," I say. "We must be gone from this place. I am surprised you made it this far. The horses are—"

I stop myself when he looks upon me with questioning eyes.

"Where did you find the horses?" I ask.

"In the woods, still tied to a wagon. You remember the trader at your brother's post?"

"Aye," I say, thinking on Mary's husband.

"His body were there too," says Ciquenackqua. "We left him for the crows and took what we could of the wagon."

My brow wrinkles. "My father was with you?"

"For a time," he says. "We should not have escaped if not for him. He found us in the night, and hastened us move on. Creek Jumper's injuries slowed us before we found the horses."

I look on our shaman, his blood painting the mare's side, and wonder if he will slow us still.

"Your father left me with Creek Jumper," says Ciquenackqua. "He told us make for your brother's post and give them warning, if we were able."

"We go there as well," I say.

"We?"

I wet my lips with my tongue. "Aye. I escaped Two Ravens and his party and took a captive of my own. A witch."

Ciquenackqua smiles. "Good. Perhaps we can trade her for my mother—"

I raise my hand to quiet him. "Two Ravens will not trade, but this witch may yet be valuable to us. She warned that others in their party journey to my brother's post."

"Then let us go now."

I shake my head. Look on the horses and their cargo.

"How badly wounded is Creek Jumper?" I ask.

"Injured, but he rides," says Ciquenackqua. "He took a potion for rest and asked me bind him to the mare. He said he did not know when he will wake."

I cut the cargo from the horses to ease their burden and make them swifter.

"Come," I take up the reins of the lead stallion, leading them and Ciquenackqua to our makeshift camp.

Mary straightens seeing us. "My husband's horses," she says. "Where did you find them?"

Ciquenackqua pauses at the sight of both women in my company and points his tomahawk at Mercy.

"She is your captive?" he asks in the tongue of our people.

"Aye." I reply in kind, seeing him swing the weapon in practice. "You have met?"

"I saw her at the battle." He grimaces. "She killed Deep River."

I fall to my knees at his words.

"His body floated down the Wah-Bah-Shik-Ka, and it swallowed him whole," says Ciquenackqua.

My tears wet the earth for the deaths and captures of my people, all at Mercy's planning. I glare at her, and see she watches me back with little regard for my mourning.

"Let me kill her now," says Ciquenackqua.

"No." My voice breaks. "She is mine to slay and at my chosen time."

His face speaks to his disapproval, yet he obliges.

"This other one you may remember from the trade post,"

I tell him. "They held her captive too and kept us separate from the others."

"Hello," Mary says to him.

Ciquenackqua dons the face of his father, cold and silent to her welcome of him.

"Let Mary ride with you on the stallion," I say to calm him. "I will take Mercy with me."

I lead my horse toward the tree, and watch Mary struggle to mount the beast.

Ciquenackqua looks on me with disgust as he, too, witnesses her failed attempts.

"Have you never ridden a horse?" I ask her.

"Not in a long while," she says, her face blustery red from her efforts. "I am used to my husband's wagon."

I shake my head then point to a fallen tree. "Ciquenackqua, take her there to mount."

He mutters curses in our people's tongue as he carries out my wishes.

Mercy chuckles as I approach. "It was not enough we had one cow among us," she says. "Now you would alert the whole forest to our presence with three horses."

I untie her from the tree and lead her to our mare.

Unlike her Salem sister, Mercy has no trouble mounting. She swings astride its back with her hands bound and little help from me.

I leap atop the horse behind her and click my tongue, ushering the mare to move on with my heels. I lead the other two at a brisk pace, though not so fast to further harm Creek Jumper, or throw Mary.

We ride all day, me forced to ride behind my sister's killer.

Her smoke scented hair breezing in my face. I think to cut it from her, but fear I should not stop with trimming it.

Come the nightfall, we stop to rest.

My mind cautions I should heed Mercy's words and keep on, but, as I look on my company, I know we cannot abandon them. Ciquenackqua appears half out of his wits, and Creek Jumper has not woken once during our ride. Our shaman sleeps still, and I think of no reason why I should take him from his horse.

I give the reins of all three mounts to Ciquenackqua as Mercy slides off behind me. Then I take her to a nearby elm and tie her off.

Tonight, she does not speak.

I reckon she knows her words useless on me and would not waste her breath. I leave her at the tree and join the others, not twenty yards away.

Mary waits awake, though Ciquenackqua has already bedded down.

I gather he must be grateful to have found me, for he snores in blissful slumber, not thinking I might have needed him take the first watch. I rub my eyes with the ball of my fist as I sit upon the grass.

I look back on Mercy, my own escape having made me warier still of Mercy's wily nature. I exhale, thankful she remains captive to the tree.

"Ah." Mary winces beside me and rubs her inner thighs.

"You will be sore for several days," I say.

"Aye," she says. "I remember the pain from my youth. Do not let me trouble you. I would not have you slowed for it."

I keep my silence rather than remind her she slowed me already by falling off her mount several times earlier in the day.

I wriggle down in the dirt, resting my head upon a stone. Then I look up at the stars and the night sky, wondering if Sarah looks down on me.

"Thank you," Mary says quietly, "for not leaving me."

I glance in her direction as she continues rubbing her thighs. She will not meet my eyes.

"I know others should have left me by now," she says. "Indeed, my own husband threatened it more than once when he were alive. I know not why God made me so fumbling, but I am grateful for your kindness."

Her gentle voice bids me scold myself for thinking ill of her.

I cannot, nor can I bring myself to lie and say she is no trouble.

"You should sleep, Mary."

"No," she says. "I slept all last night. It is you who should take rest this eve."

I shiver from the night chill and wish we might risk a fire. "I do not mind."

"Or do you not trust me?"

Her words strike me like a slap to the cheek and, for all her earlier shyness, I find her looking well on me now. Her eyes search mine, as if she could discern the truth or lie in my answer.

"I know not who to trust," I say honestly. "But I will say this. Look you on Mercy and see I keep her bound while you yet walk free."

"Aye." Mary casts her gaze away. "But that is because you fear her. No one fears one such as me."

"Why should you wish others to fear you?"

"Oh, let you not think such ill thoughts of me," she says

quickly. "I meant naught of it, only that there be strength in fear. Great power for those who wield it."

I know not what to say to her words, and gather she senses my unease for she fidgets, scratching at her arms.

"I should not expect you to understand," she says. "Look at you. Beautiful as a blooming rose, yet with thorns to prick any who dare touch you. I have envied girls like you all my life, often wondering what it must be like to have men's eyes follow me as I watched them do for Mercy and Abigail in Salem."

"I should think it because those two gave men whatever they liked," I say.

"No," she says. "It were not for that alone. I followed God's word and gave my husband whatever he asked of me, yet I never saw the desire in his eyes he had for you that day at your brother's post."

She laughs then, alarming me.

"Then again, I never saw such surprise when you near castrated him either."

I chuckle with her at that, the pair of us near waking Ciquenackqua, to judge his restlessness.

"Ah, but that were a fine sight to see," says Mary. "One I shall never forget."

My mind races back to that day, drawing a grin from me. "Nor I. My father taught me words are not enough for some men."

"He taught you well then," she says.

Her shoulders shake and her breath catches in her throat.

"Forgive me my trespasses against you, Rebecca," says Mary. "I had not thought to alert Mercy and her guards to your escape."

I sigh, not wishing her further pain, though not wishing to lie either.

"And when I saw you and him brought back..." She wipes her nose with the back of her hand, pauses to compose her voice. "I know not why God made me so weak. I have often asked Him why He hates me so."

We two sit awhile—she crying softly, me thinking on what to say.

"My sister asked the same many a night," I say finally. "Sarah was her name."

"Aye," says Mary. "Hannah spoke of you both often while we toiled at her hearth this past winter. She said your sister could not give up her guilt for the night that brought you all into these lands, much the same as Andrew Martin could not."

I nod. "She believed your god punished her for those actions."

"I thought He did the same to me for my part in Salem," says Mary. "But His scorn for me were there long before the trials. Let Mercy blather about her master, Thomas Putnam, chasing her skirt around the house. I should have welcomed such a master as he rather than the one God led me to serve."

She turns to me of a sudden, takes my hand in hers.

"I heard Mercy on the road say Putnam kept a journal. That it was in your sister's keeping for a time."

"Aye," I say. "It were given Sarah by Abigail Williams."

Mary's eyes seem round and bright as I look on them, her gaze more curious than ever I have witnessed in a person.

"And did you read it also?"

I hesitate, wondering what draws her interest so keenly. "Aye, I read the entries."

"Did he..." Mary wets her lips. "Did he ever mention my name in his writings? Do you recall that from your readings?"

"Mary—"

"Please, Rebecca," she says. "Please, I must know."

"Aye," I say. "You were mentioned somewhat."

"And?" she asks. "What did Putnam say?"

I struggle to recall the words rightly. I think back on the days Father bid me study the journal, burning each name in my head in the event there ever came such a day as this. I remember believing him foolish then, one of the only times in my life to ever think so. Yet now as I sit beside one of the Salem accusers, and look on another tied twenty yards away, I realize him all the wiser still.

"Putnam said his daughter mentioned you were eager to join the afflicted girls."

"Aye," Mary says, her voice small and quiet. "All I ever desired were for them to befriend me. I often prayed for but one kind word from them. For Mercy or Abigail to look on me with fondness, rather than lead the others in mocking me. Can you believe I thought my prayers answered the night they asked me join them in the woods?"

"You danced with them then?"

"Oh, aye," she says, her voice near bursting from the memory. "If ever I were happy a night in my life it was then when they took me by the hand and led me around the fire. I can still see their happy faces in my dreams and hear my laughter twinning theirs."

She hangs her head then, a sight to sadden me also.

"I should have known then it were all a show," says Mary. "*I did know.* Only did not care. They gave me Devil's powder, and that I took gladly. Not to see spirits," she says quickly, seeing me look on her oddly. "No. Only that it were what they would have from me in friendship...and then John Proctor took it all from me."

A dusky edge haunts her voice, one that makes me wonder if it indeed came from Mary.

"He was your master?"

"Aye. He knew the claims we gave were false and would not have me lie or risk despoiling his good name and household." Mary spits. "Much as I recall the night Mercy and Abigail asked me join them, I can recall with equal measure John Proctor's threats against me."

Mary looks on me, her face washed with grief and anger.

"Have you ever seen the glow of tongs or brands pulled from the fire?" she asks. "Heard them sizzle when pressed against an animal's hide?"

"Aye," I say. "I have helped George with his own beasts before."

Mary nods. "Imagine the man whose roof you live beneath threatening to feed those fiery tongs to you. Promising he should force them down your throat if you keep up your pretense."

"No," I say, remembering the animals' stir when I held them for George that he might brand them.

"Aye," Mary insists. "That is the horror John Proctor swore me if I did not recant."

I think on such a picture as she paints in my mind, wondering how a man could threaten such a thing to a lowly girl. Then the familiar anger swells inside at what I should do if someone gave me such a warning.

"Let Mercy and the others say what they will of me, that

I were weak and a traitor to their cause," says Mary. "But I knew Proctor well. Nothing kept him from standing by his word. That be why I gave those magistrates the truth of it."

Mary sobs anew, and I cannot help but place my arm about her broad shoulders.

"And then I were cast out," she says. "The only one to bear the hate from all sides. No more friendship from the other girls. No fear of my power from those in the village. And worse, Dr. Campbell would give me no more of his Devil's powder."

I think again on the man Sarah would name as our real father. Hearing Mary speak so of him gives me further reason to hate his shared blood flowing in my veins and that his actions warranted such loss upon so many, continuing its reach even to this night.

"Proctor beat me for what he wrongly supposed a lazy nature in me," Mary says. "But it were only agony from the lack of powder. The pain it caused me were so great I again betrayed my earlier words. I rejoined the girls not for friendship, or even to see spirits again, only that the powder should remove the pain. Would that I knew then what I do now."

"What is that?" I ask.

"That had I only endured awhile longer, the pain should leave my body and find my wits returned again," says Mary. "Though at least the second time it came upon me, I did not also have to bear Proctor's fists. I may hate Abigail and Mercy all the rest of my days, but I will be forever grateful they named Proctor a witch and that I saw his neck break for it."

I look on Mary with new understanding and not a little appreciation for the cold way she speaks of Proctor's death. It mirrors my own thoughts of how I should feel upon taking Mercy's life.

"I am glad Thomas Putnam wrote of me," says Mary quietly. "I did not think he knew my name."

Her words sadden me, that she should speak so proud of the mere mention in a stranger's journal, and even then in not a goodly light. Still, she smiles at me as I take my arm from her shoulders.

"Let you sleep now, Mary," I say. "And I will take the watch."

"Aye," she says. "If you insist."

"I do. Your body needs rest to heal the pain in your legs. We should reach my brother's post tomorrow, but it will yet be a long day's ride."

She takes my hand and brings it to her lips, kissing my knuckles. "Thank you for all your kindness."

"You are most welcome," I say. "Now, sleep. The morrow will come before we know it."

She takes her hand from mine and lies upon the ground, her snores echoing not long after,

The night sky and the star guide my Father learned me to plot and follow calls my name.

A lone wolf howls in the distance. Its echo meant to warn others of its presence, yet its sound brings me comfort.

I close my eyes and offer a prayer to the ancestors, bidding them keep safe watch over Father and our people, wherever they may be. My thoughts dwell on my companions; hate for Mercy, mourning for Ciquenackqua, and concern for Creek Jumper.

I think on Mary last, of her thanks for my kindness.

The wolf's howl echoes again, bidding me wonder if it would not be a greater kindness to grant her the silent, merciful death we gave Mercy's guards.

The moon sits directly over me ere the thought leaves me.

Then I wake Ciquenackqua and bid him keep the remainder of the nightly watch. Once assured he has fully woken, and after he wanders into the night to relieve himself, I nestle down close to Mary, feel her warmth against my back, and let sleep take me.

My dreams fill with my *manitous* and the path it would lead me down.

-thirteen-

CIQUENACKQUA SHAKES ME AWAKE. TEARS STAIN WHERE WAR paint coated his face yesterday.

I sit up, shielding my eyes as the sun peeks at me from the horizon and bids us rise with it for a new day.

"What is it?" I ask.

"Creek Jumper is dead."

I look to the white mare, and see our shaman yet tied where we left him. I climb to my feet and hurry toward the beast.

The mare spins from me. I catch its reins in hand, then soothe it with my voice and stroke its jawline. I touch my fingers to Creek Jumper's neck, finding it cold and stiff.

My feet fail me. I land hard upon the ground and gaze up into his wizened face.

His eyes closed in blissful sleep, I almost think him smiling down on me from atop his mount.

Ciquenackqua sits beside me. "So many dead," he says. "Why?"

I say nothing in reply, unable to take my eyes off our shaman.

"Did he say anything to you?" I ask. "Before he slept?"

"Only that I must continue on and his potion would make him sleep awhile, but I should not worry."

Ciquenackqua's words call more tears from me. I know full well our shaman understood that he would not wake in this life again. But even in death, Creek Jumper would not allow a boy to believe himself left alone.

"What should we do with him?" Ciquenackqua asks.

"We will take his body to the post and give it a proper burial." I hand the reins over. "Stay with him while I rouse the others."

Before leaving, I brush Creek Jumper's hair aside and kiss his cold brow, allowing my lips linger there, though it seems as if it were a stone. I offer a prayer that he not take Ciquenackqua or me with him on the spirit path, then leave them both.

I nudge Mary awake and hear her groan with morning pain.

Mercy keeps her quiet at my approach, and while I loosen her bonds. I lead her to our mount. She wrinkles her nose at the sight of Creek Jumper.

"Thought I smelled death—"

I unsheathe my father's dagger and knock Mercy over the head with its hilt.

She falls to the ground unconscious, and I find myself shaking.

"Do it," says Mary. "Or give me the blade"—her open hand reaches out to me—"and I shall do it for you."

"Ciquenackqua," I say, sheathing the dagger in my belt. "Help me lay her across my horse."

He listens without question, smirking at the sight of Mercy laid out.

"Why do you keep her alive?" Mary asks.

I look on the streak of black painting Mercy's eyes. "I would learn more from her."

I swing astride the horse. Ciquenackqua lifts her limp body while I pull, the two of us placing her across my lap.

The horse paces beneath me, seemingly eager to set off for my brother's post or else sensing the evil spirit upon its back.

Thoughts of George cloud my mind as we ride. I drive my mount harder with each passing hour, worrying what I should find at the post, wondering if Mercy spoke true, and plotting what we should do if finding the post sacked by a second raiding party.

All afternoon, I look to the horizon and hope not to find a billowing cloud of smoke.

My fears go mercifully unwarranted as I witness familiar white smoke rising from George and Hannah's chimney.

No one stands in the yard.

The dogs still wander, as do the livestock inside their fencing.

All seems well to my eye, yet I cannot fight the fear clutching my insides. My mind swarms with images of Sarah slain in the village, our people dragged away and Father with them, even Creek Jumper, dead upon our mare in our company.

I slide off my horse and give the reins over to Ciquenackqua.

"What are you doing?" he asks.

"Stay here," I say.

"Why? Where are you going?"

I do not tell him that I must know, that I must be certain what little family I have left still lives.

I sprint through the forest, drawing my tomahawk and Father's dagger from my belt. My muscles tense as I near the edge of the woods and take shelter against an oak.

I peek around the tree, but see nothing in the yard.

My heart beats faster, thankful I have not found any trace of war. Still, I worry what I might find inside the houses.

I push off the tree and make for the back of George's home. I throw myself against the side. Slowly, I raise my head and peek inside.

A rifle cocks behind me.

"Rebecca?"

George stands in the woods behind me. He sets his rifle to lean against a tree.

"Rebecca, what are you—"

I give him no time to finish his words, throwing myself into his arms, crying until I have no tears left in me.

"She is dead," I say. "S-Sarah is dead."

George pulls away. "How?"

I tell him everything, my tongue loosing a dam of words on him like I have never before spoke. All the while, he listens, never interrupting. With each bit of news I pass onto him, his face sours, his shoulders and body sagging until I fear he will fall over.

"We had no word of it," he says after I have finished. "No word at all."

"Aye," I say. "And that is why I came as quick as I were able. That I might warn you—Mercy says another party comes for us."

Rage crosses his face as he strides to the tree and takes up his long rifle, his gaze searching the surrounding area.

"When will they come?" George asks.

"I do not know," I say. "Tonight, mayhap. Tomorrow?"

"Then we should make ready for them," he says grimly. "I have more than enough powder and shot to manage all who would fight against us."

"Is Andrew here? Bishop and Hannah?"

"Aye, for all the good they will do us. An old man, a drunk, and my wife against a war party of braves and witches," says George. "It falls to you and I to fend them off, little sister."

I nod. "I bring others also, in the woods not far from here, though I fear they will be little help either."

"If they can hold a rifle and stand to post they will suffice," says George. "This will not be the first war party I've defended against. I built these grounds for such times. If they be like all the others, we will yet stand come the end."

My brother's words lend me courage as we together go to reclaim the others in my company.

"You said Priest was taken also?" he asks.

"Aye, taken that I might be free."

"Should we survive this wave, we will seek them out," says George. "Pay whatever they require to free him and the others."

I relish the idea, but fear our aid will come too late. I push aside such ill thoughts and allow myself some of the hope my brother speaks on.

"George," says Mary upon our arrival. "Oh, George, I had not thought to ever see you again."

"Nor I you," he replies. "At least not for some time. Your husband—"

Mary shakes her head.

"I shall miss him," says George. "A stubborn brute, he was, but he had a good mind for the trade."

My brother turns his attention away from her, walking to Ciquenackqua and pulling him close.

"I am sorry for your loss, brother. But I know your father would be proud that you yet live. You will do him prouder still." George roughly brushes Ciquenackqua's hair. "Now come, all of you. We have much to plan and discuss."

I bring up the rear of our group as George leads us into his yard.

"Mary, go tell Hannah what has happened," he says. "Ciquenackqua, put some food in your belly and gather what rest you can. It's man's work we do tonight, and I'll have need of you beside me. Now off you go."

Ciquenackqua smiles upon hearing my brother name him a man, a catching sight that takes hold of me also. Though I were but a girl at the time, I well remember seeing George and Andrew brighten when Bishop welcomed them into manhood with such a claim.

"What of me, brother?" I ask.

He looks on Mercy's body, still lain across the mare's back. "I would hear from this witch with my own ears. And it might be I have means of fetching truths from her that you did not."

I follow his lead into the barn and witness my father's stallion bristle at the sight of more his own kind come into his home. Together, George and I cut Creek Jumper's body free of the tethers binding him to the mare's back. We lay him gently into a mound of hay, and I cover him with a blanket. I hope the time arises where we may give him a proper burial, though my mind speaks it may never occur.

My mourning turns hateful as George brings Mercy to the ground.

He takes hold of her armpits, dragging Mercy into a stable and tethering her against a wooden post.

"What are you going to do?" I ask.

"She be the one who murdered Sarah?" he asks. "The cause of all this?"

"Aye."

George's face wrenches with pain, struggling with such emotions, as he looks down on Mercy. He leaves me alone with her and returns with a bucket full of water, throwing it full on her face.

Mercy wakes with a shriek, sputtering and spitting. She shakes wet hair from her eyes and looks around the stable then to my brother and I. "So it has come to this?" Mercy asks. "Hello, George Kelly. Have you brought me here for torture?"

"You know me?" He asks.

"Aye. You look an exact twin of your father." Mercy sneers. "And I see his coldness in your eyes."

"Good," says George. "Let you think well on it and answer my questions wisely."

"I will answer," she says. "But with little concern for whether you find them wise or no. I prefer truth."

George scratches his beard and glances at me. "Why do you come for us after so many years? Why could you not let us be?"

"This new world be a large place," she says. "Not all are so fortunate to have friends among the savages. Say instead it has taken us this long to find you and—"

George kicks her ribs with his boot, silencing Mercy.

I wince as she groans from the blow and turns her glare on him, her chest heaving, her breath wheezing.

"Speak no more lies to me, witch," says George. "Or you will receive more of the same and worse. My family and friends are but a few whites in a sea of copper out here. From what my sister says, you have native friends also. They could have found us if and when you wished. Why now?"

Mercy chuckles then coughs, clutching her ribs where George kicked her. "You are much better at this game than your sisters."

"Answer me." George growls.

"We knew you lived, aye," says Mercy. "And I should have found you easy enough, if sent out. But I am only a humble servant in this game between our fathers, as I told your sister."

"Then by all means," says George, "give me the name of whom you serve."

Mercy grins. "You already know."

"The Mathers," I say.

"Aye," says Mercy. "Though there be only one left now. The son, Cotton."

"Why should famed reverends we have never met wish us harm?" George asks.

"I do not suppose the elder Mather did," she says. "Increase protected you all, once he learned Abigail were sent out to fetch you. He bid us give up our anger and vengeance and allow the score be settled with the deaths of your father and Abigail. The lot of us mattered little to him."

I weigh her words, trying to recall all I could from the Putnam journal. "Then why does Cotton hate us so?" I ask. "What keeps his hate for us burning?"

Mercy shrugs. "Torture me all you will, but I do not know the answer. Cotton is a goodly man though. He understood my pain at the loss of Abigail and set me to find you all and end this strife."

"Such a powerful man as he would not send you out for that reason alone," says George. "There must be another reason he would see us dead."

"I suppose you right," says Mercy. "But it matters little to me. His order served my purposes well enough."

I make a show to her of looking around the stable. "Aye. He has served you well."

"Better than you know." Mercy grins in a way I like not at all. "I should not have found you without his resources, aye, and his social connections."

"Let you speak to them then," I say.

"No, sister. She knows naught," says George, lifting the hammer from his belt. "We should be done with her lying tongue now and make our preparations."

"Many things and names are what I know, George Kelly," said Mercy. "Strike me again and you will learn no more of them."

"Perhaps I should burn you then," says George. "Give you a sampling of Hell before I send you there."

An edge taints my brother's voice that I have never heard before. When Mercy shows little regard for his words, George looks to the rope and station he hangs deer to bleed them out.

"Or maybe I shall string you up like Abigail Williams did our father in the woods," says George. "That you might see your blackened guts before you leave this world."

"There is nothing you could do that has not already harmed me a thousand times over." Mercy levels her gaze on my brother. "Do your worst."

The icy way she speaks bids my body shiver, though I gather it has not affected my brother in the same manner.

"You still have all your limbs, and no missing teeth," says George. "There is much and more I could do to you that has not been done."

"Strong words," Mercy laughs. "But you are no torturer."

"Not before this day, but you will find my hand steady nonetheless," says George. "As you said, I am my father's son."

And I am my father's daughter, I think, my thoughts dwelling on Priest.

"Then you should look after your own life and flee now," says Mercy. "As your father did when learning a storm came for him."

"Our father fled Salem with a guilty conscience," says George. "Nothing more."

Mercy shakes her head. "He left for wont of his life. You should do the same, if you were wise. There's a traitor in your midst, fool. And you've been blind to it all this time."

Mercy laughs at the apparent confusion upon my face and George's.

"Can it be you still do not know where I learned of your location?" Mercy asks. "Of this trade post and your names?"

George and I say nothing, though my mind races with Mercy's mention of a traitor.

"Your friend"—Mercy grins as she looks on George—"Andrew Martin."

-fourteen-

I REEL AT MERCY'S CLAIM.

"That cannot be," I say, seeing George also confused. "Andrew loves my brother more than his own soul. He would never betray—"

"Whiskey loosens the tongues of men," says Mercy. "And a pretty face fetches more answers still."

"No." I shake my head. "You lie."

"Do not name me liar," Mercy says, her voice rising. "Would you have more proof from me? Let you ask Andrew of his bride to be, Susannah Barron."

George flinches beside me.

"Ah. Does it surprise you I know her name?" Mercy asks. "Let that speak to my truth."

"How do you know her?" I ask.

"Who should have guessed a little bird from my past would spawn another to aid me in the present," says Mercy. "It seems only natural a daughter of my Salem sister came to me, especially with news of her engagement to a fiancé hailing from the wilderness."

My face pales at her words.

"Oh," says Mercy. "But do not take my word for it. After all, you both yet think me a liar. Might I suggest you bring Andrew here?" She sneers. "Let the truth of his face speak plain the moment he sees me among you."

"Aye," says George. "I would judge the truth of it in such a manner."

George storms out of the stable so quickly that he does not witness the smirk draw across Mercy's lips as I do.

I chase after him, catching my brother before he leaves the barn.

"What are you doing?" I whisper.

"Finding him," he says. "If Andrew truly led her here…if Sarah and the others in your village died because of him—"

"But what if Mercy is lying?" I ask. "Perhaps all her actions and words distracts us from preparing for war against Two Ravens and the second war party she spoke of."

George sighs. He runs his hand through his hair then shakes his head. "Perhaps she does," he says finally. "But I must learn the truth of it."

He leaves me to guard Mercy.

Turning back to the barn, I wonder if I should revisit her. My thoughts wander to Andrew, fearing what it will mean if she spoke true of him, wondering what George would do to him. Worse still, what I might do.

I watch from afar as George knocks on Bishop's door. Seeing the old man appear in the entry stabs my heart. We must tell him of Sarah soon too, though my mind warns it will not take him long to know the truth of it upon seeing me again so soon and us preparing defenses.

My palm brushes the hilt of Father's dagger, and I find myself walking toward the stable.

"Back so soon?" Mercy asks me. "One might begin to wonder if you and I are drawing close to one another."

"The only time I will draw close to you is—"

"Yes, yes, I know," she says. "To kill me and take my pretty hair."

I glare at her returning my hate with a spiteful grin.

"Still, you have had many a chance now and not done so," says Mercy. "Why?"

"Do you hate living so that you would tempt me?"

"No," she says. "I much prefer life. But my curious nature would understand your reasons. I said you and I are much alike, yet now I doubt myself."

"Perhaps I think you yet have some little value left," I say. "Though it lessens as time passes."

"Then you grow wiser," says Mercy. "But you are also foolish. I should never have brought you to stir chaos within my own home on the eve of war." She grins at me. "Then again, you are no product of Salem."

"What does that mean?" I ask.

"Cotton chose me wisely," says Mercy. "He sees talents in people and recognized mine in Salem, furthering them after. Place me where you will, girl. Whether at church in Boston, supping in the wild with savages"—she holds her bindings up in a mocking show—"or tied in the enemy's stable, I find a way to prove my worth."

"Your worth runs low."

"Perhaps," she says. "But you shall need my talents yet when Two Ravens comes to claim vengeance on you and yours."

I look out the stable when hearing my brother and Andrew approach, though both are yet far off.

"I would ask your forgiveness, Rebecca," says Mercy, her ears also pricked in their direction. "For the lie I earlier told you."

Curiosity takes hold of me. I spin back to her, my face plain in question for the lie she speaks of.

"I told your brother he were better at this game than you," says Mercy. "That were proved wrong the moment he left to search out Andrew Martin. George would have done well to listen to you—"

I alter my gaze between her and George. Nearing the barn, grimness clouds his face that seems to surprise Andrew also. Bishop hobbles behind them, and I wonder for what purpose he comes.

"It were a small seed I planted in your brother's mind," says Mercy. "Now you will see it watered and blooming."

My tongue cannot form the words to halt George as they round the stable corner. He guides Andrew through first, keeping careful watch of Andrew's face.

"What is this you would have me see, Geor—" Andrew's eyes round at the sight of Mercy and me. "Mercy?"

George grabs Andrew by the collar of his shirt, and flings him against the stable wall. My brother draws his knife and puts it to Andrew's throat.

Andrew shrinks at the blade. "What are you doing?"

"Quiet," George says. "You listen to me now, Andrew."

The confusion in Andrew's face cautions me step forward. "Brother, let you stop this—"

"I said quiet," George says, turning his gaze back to Andrew. "Answer me, and let you be honest."

"I have ever been honest with you," says Andrew. "What cause would I have to lie?"

"How do you know this woman?" George jerks his head toward Mercy.

Andrew's mouth works wordlessly, and I near doubt he can speak at all.

"Come now, Andrew," says Mercy. "You and I—"

"Rebecca, keep her quiet," George yells.

I move to obey his command, kneeling beside Mercy and drawing my own blade to her throat. Her throbbing veins beckon me, and I think how easy it would be to end this now and let my brother gain his senses without further plots from her. Instead, I hold my blade ready, awaiting George's command.

"What is the meaning of this?" Andrew asks. His voice pained with concern.

"How do you know this woman?" asks George.

I think Andrew dazed, he looking from Mercy to George as if puzzled. "It be Susannah's Aunt Mercy," he says. "You know well my bride's mother and father did not approve of us courting, George. When they were in a foul mood, Susannah often bid us meet at her aunt's home so we might be alone with one another."

"You stayed with this woman?" George points to Mercy.

"Aye, many a night," says Andrew. "She were always kind enough to take me in."

I look on Mercy, and think her happy as a tomcat with a mouse between its teeth.

"And you," my brother's voice breaks. "You told her of us? Of our family?"

Andrew looks from me to George. "Aye."

My brother's shoulders sag and his knife drops from Andrew's throat.

"What?" Andrew asks, bewildered. "She often asked of my kin and trade."

George releases his dagger, dropping it into the straw. He backs away as one dazed. "You have killed us all," he whispers.

Andrew looks to me. "What is this?"

I shake my head and sigh, turning my gaze from Andrew.

"Mercy?" he asks. "What are you doing here?"

"You have killed us all," George's voice rises.

"I don't understand," says Andrew.

My brother has Andrew off his feet and pinned against the wall before I can think to stop him.

"You have killed us all!" George rages, his face blistery red. Tears streaming down his cheeks. "My sisters, me, and my... my wife..."

"George, I—"

"You have kill—"

"That's enough, lad!"

Bishop leans against the stable. He wipes his brow with the back of his forearm, then wheezes as he looks on all of us each in turn, stopping on George and Andrew.

"That one's yer brother," says Bishop to George. "I know yer angry and ye've a right to be. It's a damned fool what runs his mouth off to strangers, especially old hens who've nothing to do but blather on about the tales they've learned."

"Bishop—"

"No, ye listen to me now, lad," says Bishop to George. "Let him go."

My soul cries for the pain in George's eyes, the confusion in Andrew's face.

"The pair of ye are brother's," says Bishop. "In soul, if not in blood. Remember that night so long ago and all he did for ye and yer family then. Know he'll do the same again if they come this night for us."

My brother's hesitation leads me believe he may well thrash Andrew.

"He loves ye, lad," says Bishop quietly. "Loves ye with everything in him, else he'd have eaten a bullet from the end of his rifle long ago."

My brother trembles as he releases Andrew and backs away to the opposite side of the stable, collapsing.

"I don't understand," says Andrew. "What did I—"

"Damn ye to Hell, lad, shut yer fool mouth," says Bishop. "Yer the one what led this Mather bitch here." He looks on Mercy. "Isn't he?"

"Aye," she says. "But you speak true, old man. Andrew does indeed love this family with all his heart."

I glare at her, even as she continues to speak.

"You will have further need of him to live out the night," says Mercy. "As you shall also have need of me."

"We've no use for wenches here," says Bishop.

"Perhaps not," says Mercy. "But by my count, the witches I left behind to hunt down any who escaped us will arrive here this eve, if they stuck true to commands."

"If and perhaps," Bishop grunts. "I've some of me own to share with ye. If some of yer powder-snortin' bitches and savage lovers happen to come here, then perhaps I'll get me wish to kill more of them."

I grin at the conviction in his voice, the edge of a thrill I have not heard in him for many years.

"There will be more of them and to spare, old man," says Mercy. "They will overrun this place."

"Well, now." Bishop limps closer to her, putting a hand to his ear. "I don't hear the banshee wailin' me name just yet. Methinks I'll be around a lil longer. Though it's a shame ye won't be seein' yer friends tonight."

"You would be wise to trade me," she says.

"I'd be wise to string yer lyin' carcass up in the middle of the yard," says Bishop. "Hang a dead crow and ye scare off the others. Think it might work for witches, lass?"

"Aye," I reply.

Mercy looks me in the face. "You have kept me alive for a reason and know well what heads this way. Cotton ordered only that I bring back the offspring of Simon Campbell." Her eyes flit to George. "Give me to my people and let you and your brother come with me to Boston."

"Why would I do that?"

"Because I will see to it the others here will live," says Mercy. "Andrew, Hannah, the savage boy, and even this old man."

"Don't ye be listenin' to her, lass," says Bishop. "A bleedin' harpie in disguise is all she is."

I stare into Mercy's eyes and the black painted line across them. I think on my *manitous,* of Mercy's earlier words she adapts to each situation, and what such words might mean for my family and I now. What lessons I might learn from her.

"What of Two Ravens?" I ask. "You said he comes for us also."

"Aye," she says. "Have you ever heard it said, 'The enemy of my enemy is friend to me,' girl?"

I nod.

"Good," says Mercy. "Agree to my terms. Swear that you and your brother will follow me to Boston should we survive, and my people will fight alongside yours against Two Ravens and his men."

"The words of a lyin' Salem wench," says Bishop. "What's that worth?"

I turn and look on him, and George and Andrew also. I think of Sarah and the night Hecate came for us, how my family lives only thanks to her sacrifice.

I study Mercy's face, thinking on the night she destroyed my village. Of Two Ravens and all his men.

"You will not fight," I tell her. "I would have you beside me the whole battle, bound and gagged, to keep your witches loyal."

Mercy's eyes glitter with my words, even as she seems to ponder them. "They will fight and die for me," she says. "And when the dead lie in the dust and we three remain, swear that you and George will go to Boston."

"I swear it," I say.

Mercy flinches, as if I mean to trick her. "Swear it on your sister's soul."

I take the blade from Mercy's throat, run it over her hand, and draw blood. Then I do the same to my own, slicing my palm, watching both hers and mine ooze red.

I grip Mercy's hand tight, letting our blood mix, binding my pact.

"I swear it on the good soul of my sister, Sarah," I say. "We will go to Boston and meet your master."

"Then it is done," says Mercy.

"Aye," I say. "It will be."

I release my hold on her and take my leave of the stable. The others follow me out of the barn, out of hearing distance. One of them grabs my shoulder, spins me to face them.

George narrows his eyes. "What did you do? She will betray us—"

"I know what she is," I say. "And what we are not. Believe me when I say that we cannot defeat Two Ravens and his men with us alone."

"But, Rebecca," George says. "If—"

"I were there, George," I say. "Watched them take our village. And Ciquenackqua saw them defeat Father and our men on the shore of Wah-Bah-Shik-Ka. We shall need all the help we can if we are to survive this."

Andrew helps Bishop along, the pair of them joining us. "I daresay yer sister's right in this, lad."

"How can you speak so?" George asks. "You have ever been one for the fight, Bishop."

"Aye. That I have," says Bishop. "But I'm an old man now and not like to survive much longer anyway. I daresay that I won't be of much help this time around."

"We yet have three of us," says George. "And Ciquenackqua."

"It will not suffice," I say. "Even with Bishop's tricks and your rifles."

George folds his arms. "I will not go to Boston, Rebecca. No matter if Mercy keeps her word or not. Let the pair of you remember it were you who swore the oath. Not I."

"We must survive the night first," I say. "Then let us worry about what oaths I swore. For now, we should make ready our defenses."

"You seem to have a plan already." George grimaces. "Would you make it to known to us, little sister?"

"Aye." I look to the cabins. "Have Mary load all the rifles and Hannah store caches of powder and shot in each house.

Let Ciquenackqua make fires in each of their hearths and fetch enough wood to keep them burning."

Bishop grins. "You'd have them think there's more of us then?"

"Aye."

"Andrew, bar the windows and doors," says George. "We have enough timber to make short work of it. I'll be along presently to help you. I would tell Hannah all that's happened."

"A-aye," says Andrew. "George…I never…"

"Let you make no apologies here and now," says my brother. "We need work done and little time to accomplish it."

"Aye," says Andrew, slipping away to attend the task set him.

Andrew leaves us, glad, no doubt, for a reason to leave our company for a time and think on his actions.

"How am I to forgive him?" George asks.

"Me father oft said time heals many a thing," says Bishop. "Less'n it's some foul disease a whorin' wench gave ye. So steer clear of 'em."

He laughs himself into a coughing fit, one I should join in with him, if I did not recognize the darkness in my brother's eyes.

"But his sin were betrayal," says George.

"He wouldn't be here, lad, if it were true betrayal." Bishop claps him on the shoulder. "Come now. Let you go tell your wife and the others our plan."

"She'll not be happy," says George, eyeing his and Hannah's cabin.

"No doubt," says Bishop. "Most married women aren't. And who can blame 'em? Married to poor bastards like us, eh? Let ye tell her anyway."

George hesitates, despite Bishop urging him on. "Where will

you be, little sister? I heard no mention of what you mean for yourself in this."

I open my mouth to speak, but Bishop guesses my intent and says it for me.

"She'll be out rangin' then, won't she," he says. "Just as I'd have sent Priest to do."

George looks on me with little regard. "You can't. What if—"

"I move more silent than you, brother," I say.

"I cannot allow it," says George. "If Mercy's witches or the natives await—"

"I have killed more natives and witches in the last two days than you in the past ten years." I step close to my brother that he might learn truth from my eyes. "And I led others here and brought us a captive in tow. Your trade is in hoarding and bargaining weapons and pelts. Mine is using those weapons to hunt such creatures and bring their skins to you."

My brother steps back.

"I am your younger sister, it is true," I say. "But I am not helpless."

My brother's jaw works back and forth. "No," he says finally. "I see that now. In truth, you have not been for many years."

George touches his hand to my shoulder. I return the gesture.

"Keep safe, Rebecca," he says.

"And you. I will return."

As my brother leaves us, my mind berates me for speaking to him so, out of turn and disrespectfully. Still, my spirit soars that I spoke truth and he were man enough to accept it.

"And me, lass?" Bishop asks. "What would ye set an old wily bastard like me to do?"

"What you do best," I say. "String Mercy up so the witches see her when they come to shore."

"And if they don't do as she bids, I'll kill her, eh?"

"Aye."

He laughs himself into a coughing fit then. As he marches toward the barn, I sprint for the forest, hearing him sing a refrain from his favorite tune.

'Come on, lad,' says I. 'We'll hunt us some witches.'
All o'er we went and by God killed us them bitches.

-fifteen-

THE SUN DESCENDS ON THE HORIZON AS I STALK THROUGH THE wilderness, circling the edges of my brother's property.

Hammering echoes wander throughout the dale from George and Andrew attending their tasks. The sound travels far and wide, and I harbor little doubt any native presence near will recognize it for the noise of white men.

My eyes flit from tree to tree, ever in search of movement and danger.

Gripping the handles of my weapons, no small part of me hopes Two Ravens does come for me. My conscience reminds he might use my love for Father and Numees against us.

I think of Father's teachings, recall his willingness in the woods that I should run free while he returned to certain capture. Even now, I wonder if I could make the same sacrifice.

Thoughts of Father comfort me. It would please him to see me ranging, as he often did, and make him happier still that I carried his blade rather than let Mercy claim it.

I glance down at the Alden name upon its blade, wishing I could take it for my own as his adopted daughter.

A cracking branch ahead pulls the thought from me.

I duck low at the sound, slink behind a rocky outcropping, and peek around its stony edge to learn whether animal or man makes such a noise.

Ahead, the painted skin of a native brave captures my attention.

Not so young as Ciquenackqua, but not so old as me. Red paints his upper body and shaved head, and silverworks bead his ears. A plume of hawk feathers are tied in his hair, each sent out in different ways. He carries a bow slung across his back, and it is then I see what he carries in hand—a bone-hilted dagger with two ribbons, one black, the other red.

He halts of a sudden, and looks the way he came, almost as if he senses my presence.

I tuck behind the outcropping, count to three before risking another peek.

The brave moves on, walking toward my brother's post.

I grit my teeth and follow him. I move from tree to tree in cautious haste, all the while keeping alert to the sights and sounds in the forest, careful not to become prey to any of his fellows that may lurk about.

I speed myself close on him the nearer we approach the trade post.

Already I spy the back of Bishop's home—nailed boards claim the windows, though George and Andrew left some little opening for any shooter inside.

The brave gives the cabin little regard, wandering closer.

My gaze drops to the dagger in his hand. Seeing its ribbon flutter calls memories of Sarah and Mercy, knowing the dagger as their means of marking the houses.

I rush forward with little thought, screaming a war cry.

The brave spins toward me, his face plain with he had no thought of being followed.

Knocking him to the ground before he can react, I step on his wrist and hold the edge of my tomahawk to his face. "Drop your dagger."

He looks at me confused, and utters words foreign to my ear.

It matters little. Father taught me long ago all men understand one universal language. I lean forward on the brave's wrist, my added weight sending the message.

The brave releases his dagger.

I step away and bid him rise with my tomahawk. The look he gives surprises me—not one of anger or ill intent, but genuine confusion. I cannot rightly determine why, whether he be so confused by my taking him unawares, or else another point unknown to me.

I keep my eye upon him as I kneel and pick up the bone dagger. Sheathing it through my belt, I look to the other cabins. Smoke rises from each of their chimneys, the filtered light glowing through cracks in the boarded windows.

A shiver runs through me at the ruse we mean to fool Two Ravens with. I only pray it works.

The brave continues his watch of me, and he follows my gaze to the cabins.

"Move." I point the way ahead, urging him forward with the end of my tomahawk.

His fearlessness to enter an enemy camp without hassle cautions me to glance over my shoulder. Concern draws over my face as we leave the woods, fear that I have missed something, though my eyes find no trace of a clue.

I usher my captive around the cabin and find my family and friends still toiling away at their tasks—all but Bishop. He has tied Mercy to a pole in the middle of the yard and sits nearby, the point of his rifle aimed at her head.

"Ah, what's this?" He asks upon my approach. "Where did ye find this hound?"

"Sniffing around your home," I say. "He had this on him."

I show the bone dagger in my belt.

Mercy's eyes go round as she wriggles upon the pole. "They are here then."

"I saw no one else—"

"Nor should you," she says. "This one you've found belongs to Two Ravens, a scout to learn your defenses, no doubt. The others will be here soon." Mercy looks to the tree line. "You would be wise to free me now."

Bishop laughs himself into a coughing fit. "Not likely."

My Native hostage looks at us each then speaks in his foreign tongue.

"What's he blatherin' on about then?" Bishop asks.

"I do not know," I say. "I—"

"He wishes to know why this white woman is tied up."

I turn at the familiar voice.

Creek Jumper leans on Ciquenackqua for support. Poultices bind the wounds upon his chest and neck, yet life burns in his wizened face.

"You—you're alive." I fight the sudden tears in my eyes. "How?"

"The grandfathers would have me repay the wrongs done our people," he says. "Their potion made me sleep long and healed my wounds. They bid me return to guide you on that yet to come. Are we all that remains?"

"Aye," I say. "Your son..."

Creek Jumper raises his hand, silencing me. "Linnipinja gave me back my son as a babe. I thank the water panther for the many years he allowed me keep Deep River at my side. Now he walks the spirit path. It might be some of us should join him soon," Creek Jumper says. "But it will not be this night."

Creek Jumper speaks to our hostage in the unfamiliar tongue.

"You understand him?" I ask.

Creek Jumper nods. "He is a Wyandot warrior and claims the Iroquois asked his tribe to hunt for the rogue Mohawk war chief, Two Ravens, who would break the peace between their tribes by raiding without leave."

Our hostage points at Mercy and mumbles in his language.

"And the white women traveling with them," says Creek Jumper. "He asks why we have this woman bound."

"Your hostage lies," says Mercy. "Let you kill him now."

"Be silent, wench," says Bishop.

My mind swirls with the opposing stories from the native and Mercy. "Creek Jumper," I say. "Let you tell him this woman killed my sister, and were wed to Two Ravens."

"Liar." Mercy's lip curls as Creek Jumper relays my words. "I were never married to that heathen, nor should I ever have been."

I pay her no mind, my focus on the discussion between Creek Jumper and the native hostage.

"He says his people have traveled far to find Two Ravens," says Creek Jumper. "He said also the war party passed near their village. They left some of their people fighting evil spirits and craving potion given them by white women."

"Do not believe him, Rebecca," said Mercy. "Did Two Ravens himself not come among you at your own village? No doubt this one's master sent him as another wolf in sheep's clothing. Keep him at your peril, I warn you."

I look from the hostage brave to her, wondering how I might learn the truth of either. The stern features of the native remind me of a younger Sturdy Oak, his inherent stoic nature. There be no lie in his eyes, nor do I sense he bears us ill will. Still, Mercy's words also bring truth—Two Ravens did indeed come among my people fearlessly and lead them astray.

The end of Bishop's rifle wanders toward the brave's back, and the old man's eyes speak that I need only give him a word to carry out the action.

My gaze wanders over the native's body. Few scars line him, though many tattoos. One adorning his left pectoral catches my eye—the drawn animal lay on its back, its black eyes staring at me from behind its dark mask, and its ringed-tail draped between its legs, hanging down the brave's abdomen.

"Wait," I say to Bishop. "Creek Jumper, look at the marking on his chest."

Our shaman peers close at the tattoo then converses with the brave.

"He claims the ringed-tail as his *manitous*," says Creek Jumper.

Bishop cocks his rifle. "Then he be a tricksome bastard."

"Perhaps," I say to him, my gaze turning to our shaman. "But a wise man told me the ringed-tail wears many masks, and I should not mistake them for an evil nature."

The smile Creek Jumper gives me is small, but there.

I step forward and pat the brave down, feeling for any hidden weapons. Finding none, I move back. "Ciquenackqua, bind this brave and take him to Bishop's cabin."

Ciquenackqua addresses my command quickly, and he tugs the bonds tight.

The hostage bravely gives no indication of the pain it serves him.

The look Ciquenackqua gives me upon finishing the task warns he disapproves of my decision. He pushes the hostage toward the cabin and follows after.

"Wait. I will go too," says Creek Jumper. "I would learn more from this man."

I think it wise he accompanies Ciquenackqua. Even before they reach the cabin, my friendly rival's shoulders relax as Creek Jumper's calming approach works its magic upon him.

"Yer keepin' him alive then, lass?" Bishop asks.

"Aye."

"You are a fool, girl," says Mercy.

"Perhaps," I say to her. "But you yet live because of it."

I leave them both, not wishing to hear more doubts of my decision. My feet lead me to the trade post cabin where Andrew and George finish boarding the last of the windows. Inside, I find multiple rifles leaning by the window with shot and powder in easy reach beside them.

I look between the cabins, shielding my eyes from the fading sun's rays. My brother's wisdom is not lost upon me as I note the field of timber cleared, granting us easy sight of any who would cross into our domain.

A piercing whistle calls my attention, and the last hammer falls. George drops the tool inside the cabin. He exits to meet me in the yard, leaving Andrew behind to further stock it for war.

"Come back when the hard labor is finished, do you?" George asks.

"Aye. You know me too well." I point to the cabins. "You think all is prepared?"

"We shall see come the nightfall, if Mercy spoke true," he says. "How did your ranging fare?"

I look to the woods and Bishop's cabin, wondering what tales or truths Creek Jumper may coax from the brave I captured.

"They will come," I say.

"You found traces of them then?"

"Aye," I say, though I do not mention the scout for fear of George also flying into a rage at my keeping such a hostage alive. "You said this would not be the first time you've warded off raiders. Where would you position us?"

"I have thought long on that." He runs his hand through his hair. "I think it best we keep two to each cabin, allowing both persons inside to fire until the loaded rifles are spent, then one may shoot while the other loads. I built the post in such a way that with enough men, we could protect ourselves in all directions."

"A sound plan," I say. "Unless they break through us."

"Aye," says George tiredly. "And if we had two to spare in each cabin. I count only seven among us and of those seven my wife is not the best shot, nor Mary either from what she would tell."

I think back on Mary slipping among the witches, slaying them in their sleep.

"She will make good of herself," I say. "But keep her with someone of stronger resilience to stay her fear."

"Aye, Andrew, perhaps," he says. "I intend to stand with my wife in our home. That leaves you or Ciquenackqua to hold the lone position."

"No, we can make do with two per cabin. Creek Jumper yet lives."

George's face pales. "What say you? He were dead when we pulled him from the horse."

I shake my head. "His magic runs deep."

"I pray he bestows it on all our heads then." George chuckles.

"Aye," I say. "Let us hope. I would have him and Ciquenackqua take the barn and guard against the shoreline. I will stay with Bishop."

"You mean that you would keep your hostage close," says George.

I fight to keep back my grin. "Do not pretend to know me, brother."

He throws his arm around my neck and pulls me close. "I know that I am fearsome hungry, little sister. If I die this night, it will not be on an empty stomach. Come." George pulls me toward his cabin. "Let us go and eat. Night falls upon us."

I glance back to the trade cabin.

Andrew sits atop a keg barrel, his rifle in hand, eyes searching out the boarded window.

"I will be along," I say to George.

My brother's face sours at seeing my watch of Andrew. "Let him be alone with his demons, Rebecca," he says. "I told him well what his actions cost us. Much as I would like to tell him more of my pain, I think he visits it upon himself twice over. Leave him to it."

With a heavy heart, I follow George to his cabin. As I cross into his home, the scent of food warns I had been hungrier than first I realized. Hannah paces the floor while Mary sits at the table, ladling soup from her near empty bowl with crumbled remains of browned bread.

Hannah's bowl sits mostly full, and I think my sister-in-law has aged since last I saw her. Tears stream her cheeks when she looks up and sees me in the door. She leaves the table of a sudden to embrace me in her own kitchen.

"Thank God you are safe, Rebecca," she says.

"Aye," I say. "And you."

"Mary has told me all that befell you in the wilderness," says Hannah. "How you both came to such an end, I..."

"All will be well again in time, sister," I say. "We yet live."

Hannah places her hand gently to my cheek. "Aye. That we do."

"Come, wife," says George, placing his arm round her waist. "Let us eat."

"Aye, husband." Hannah wipes her tears away, then hurries toward the kettle to ladle George and me steaming bowls of stew.

I sit beside Mary at the table and reach for a hunk of brown bread, tearing an end off for myself. We eat in meager silence and speak naught of the looming threat. The stew burns my tongue, but warms my throat and insides as I swallow.

Several times, George and Hannah cast furtive looks upon one another. My brother finishes his first bowl and leans over to kiss her brow before filling his bowl again.

"Why must it come to this?" Hannah asks, her voice breaking. "Why does God punish us so?"

"Because you welcomed me into your home," says Mary quietly.

I look up from munching a bit of bread, and find Mary stares into her bowl.

"Trouble has followed me ever since my days in Salem," she says. "Me fleeing from one place to the next. If I had stayed... stayed but one time and allowed Mercy and the others have their vengeance, then perhaps none of this should have occurred."

"These witches do not come for you alone, Mary Warren," I say. "The Mathers have searched for us many years on account of our blood father."

"Aye," says Mary, her gaze happening upon my brother. "I-I thought to tell you all when first I saw your face, George."

"Why?" He asks.

"You look so much like your father," she says. "In truth, I near thought you a ghost risen from my past to torment me. I warned my husband we should leave, but he would not hear it. Not with the last year's winter approaching. Forgive me, for it were fear of my husband's hand that kept me silent then."

Mary shakes her head, sniffle back her tears.

"And when I spent time among you, learned of your great kindness here in this very kitchen, I…"

Hannah reaches out to take Mary's hand in hers. "It is all right, Mary."

"No." Mary recoils. "No, it isn't. I am a coward, Hannah. I should have warned you all, and yet I did nothing. I found myself torn the day my husband led us from here and still I did not tell you. You each should have cast me out like Mercy and my Salem sisters for the wrongs I have done you all."

"You will make them right tonight, Mary," I say. "By standing with us."

"A-aye," she says. "That I will."

I smear the last bits of stew upon the remaining bread and swallow it whole, wiping my lips with the back of my hand as I stand.

"You wished to know why the Mathers have hunted you all these years," says Mary.

I pause and look from her to George, all of us in surprise at her words. "Aye."

"Their legacy," she says. "In all my years of serving men, even those of humble origins are concerned with the name they leave behind. All wish the acts they have done will live on. I saw my master John Proctor hang for his when he would not give the lie we asked of him. He cared more for his legacy than his own life. If such a man as he cared for his own name, what do you think men as powerful as the Mathers would do to keep theirs in good standing?"

"I do not understand," I say.

"Any who defy them are put down," says Mary. "Aye, even their allies. Look you to Salem and you will see it true. Most who played a part in bringing Salem to its knees paid with their lives. The Putnams are long dead, even their daughter Ann who were one of my Salem sisters. Did you know she asked forgiveness for her part in Salem?"

"No," I say.

"Aye," says Mary. "Told all who would listen she believed those we accused were innocent. She died not many years after that confession. I heard others claim her death of strange circumstance, but I know it were at the Mather's bidding. She called the trials into question with her plea and were silenced for it."

Mary looks up from her bowl. "Oh, she were not alone in being quieted. The same could be said of my other Salem sisters also. They killed Susannah Sheldon not long after the trials ended, aye, and Martha Sprague too, though she changed her name and went into hiding as I did. I knew then they would never stop hunting for me. I, the one who betrayed their cause most."

"Not the most," I say. "Our blood father did that."

"Aye," says George. "And now I think him all the wiser for it."

"I do not," I say. "Sarah often mentioned your god believes men reap what they sow. I say our blood father earned his death."

"How can you say that?" George asks, his voice cold and hard.

"Because I face truth."

George rises from the table. "He was our father, Rebecca, whether you like it or no."

"No," I say. "A true father keeps his children safe and does naught to bring them harm."

"Husband," says Hannah softly, reaching for him.

George pulls his hand away from her. "Then let you speak more truth, sister. These witches hunt Priest for his name also."

My cheeks redden at his tone.

"The same man you name father brought these witches after him"—George steps closer—"and on Sarah and your village."

I slap him without thinking then feel his hands upon my shoulders as he lifts me from the ground.

"Stop it, George!" Hannah screams. "Stop it!"

George flings me aside as his wife beats upon his back. He ignores her, glaring at me on the floor. "I will not have you speak ill of our dead father," he says. "I have tolerated your hate for him all these years, but I will not suffer it any longer."

Tears sting my eyes at my brother's words, seeing him in such a state as I have never before seen.

"Like it or no, he gave us life, sister," says George. "And it were a good one until these witches stole it from us. Let them and that malicious Putnam convince you otherwise, but I *knew* our father's heart." His voice quivers. "Whatever they say of him, he were a good man to us and would dote on you still if not for their scorn."

I pick myself off the floor.

Mary sits quiet at the table, not daring to look any of us in the eye.

I glance back at George. "Brother, I—"

"*Father loved you, Rebecca.*" George sputters the words as tears fall naked down his cheeks. "You most of all, though I should have done all I could to please him. I never hated you for it, as Sarah did, but let you speak no more ill of our father, sister, or God save me I will thrash you for it."

George's words sting more than any blade I have ever been cut with. Hannah embraces him, and his shoulders tremble at her touch.

Not knowing what to say, I run from their cabin and out to the barn, falling upon the loose straw to weep what tears my body kept back. My mind unlocked and memories flooded of the man I once knew and called Father.

I think of the life before and the old words. The familiar prayers we offered up in times of need. Two words haunt me more than any other, and yet they are the only two I can think to utter now.

"F-forgive me," I cry to his soul. "Forgive me, Father."

-sixteen-

I KNOW NOT HOW LONG I LAY IN THE STRAW, BUT NIGHT SURrounds me when I rise. I leave out of the barn and find smoke yet rises from the chimneys of all the cabins. The fire burning in the middle of the yard intrigues me most.

Mercy remains bound to a post near the fire, she seeming asleep.

Ciquenackqua sits near her. His gaze rests on the flames, though he looks back at me as I approach him.

"What are you doing out here?" I ask.

"Bishop needed rest, and I needed peace."

"As do we all," I say. "But we must make ready now. None can know the hour when Mercy's witches or Two Ravens and his men will attack."

Ciquenackqua nods, though elsewise I gather he has not heard me at all. "You dance well," he says finally. "Before we left for war, I asked the grandfathers how is it a squaw may dance better than the son of Whistling Hare. Do you bring me their answer now, daughter of Black Pilgrim? That I might know it before I die."

He looks me full in the face, all his proudness gone.

"I bring no answer," I say to him.

"I know you saw me in the woods that morning," he says. "I thought at first you came to mock me."

"I thought to," I say in earnest. "But recognized you banished yourself to the woods for such a matter rather than risk mockery."

"Aye," he says. "And from my father. Do you come to mock me now?"

"You will hear naught of that sort from me, son of Whistling Hare," I say, sitting beside him. "Do you think yourself the first to practice the dance, alone? I myself have done so many times."

He thinks me tricksome, to judge the look on his face.

"Why should you need practice?" he asks. "You dance better than any I have ever seen. Even than your father."

My words catch on my tongue. I think back on Ciquenackqua's movements. It strikes me he did not imitate Father, more that he danced in a way to mirror my own.

"It is a woman's grace she should move better than men," I say.

"Why?" he asks. "What need does a girl or woman have to make the war dance?"

"The same reason as you," I say. "I would make my father proud."

Ciquenackqua's chin dips. "At least you saw it from him that night. I shall never see it from my own now."

I glance up to the stars above. "You do not think he looks down on you? Led you to find me in the wilderness that we might come here together?"

"I think he would be ashamed I ran from the battle."

"I know this may be small comfort," I say. "But at least he thought you worthy to accompany him."

Ciquenackqua grins at me, then frowns when he sees the necklace I still wear.

"I remember when Father gave that to me." He picks up

a pebble, rolling it in his hands. "Said that he crafted a shell every year on the day of my birth. All so he could give it to me when I learned my *manitous*." He tosses the pebble into the fire. "Even that did not please him."

"But you saw the great snapper," I say.

"No," he says. "A pair of painted turtles only, one small and the other large. Both crawled from the river, but the larger hid in its shell when a white man approached. The smaller bit the white man and scared him off. Father later asked me tell everyone both turtles were snappers. Slow creatures, but with powerful bites."

I reach for the ends of the necklace and untie it, rubbing my fingers across the shells a final time before handing it over.

"No," says Ciquenackqua. "I cannot take it. My father commanded me give it to you that I might learn wisdom. That I should think before I speak and act."

"You have learned that lesson now," I say, insisting he take it. "Let you wear it as a reminder. Not of the lesson, but the care and time your father took in carving the shells."

Ciquenackqua takes the necklace from me. He rolls the shells in his hand, listening to them *clack* together. "Father said I could learn much from my *manitous*. See the raised edges on this side of the shell, and the smooth on the other?"

He holds the shells before the fire that I might better know his meaning.

"Father said we men are like this also. Each of us having our sharp and gentle sides." He grins. "I never understood the sharp in me until I saw him fall at the river. Now my spirit rages in wonder if I should ever feel the gentle side again."

He dons the necklace and ties it off, his fingers flipping each shell to ensure the smooth sides touch his chest.

"Father told me he often regretted his own nature," says Ciquenackqua. "That he struggled with acting first and thinking later. He wished me different."

"And so you are," I say. "You are the little turtle that bit."

"No," he says. "Even when I woke from the dream fast I knew that I were the larger one. The meeker."

"You are the larger—"

Ciquenackqua and I wheel upon hearing the voice behind us, finding Creek Jumper slipped among us silently. He holds a folded wolf pelt in one hand, a bowl filled with liquid in the other, and a small drum tucked beneath his arm.

"But you are not meek, son of Whistling Hare," says Creek Jumper. "When I were a boy, the old ones said sons take after their grandfathers. I think the little turtle in your dream fast will keep well alive the fighting spirit of his grandfather, Whistling Hare, and temper it with the patient wisdom of his father...you, Ciquenackqua."

Creek Jumper lays his pelt and drum upon the ground. Then approaches us with his bowl of liquid that shines black in the firelight.

"But that is the future," he says. "And we must live in the present now."

Creek Jumper offers up his voice, singing the old songs as he dips two fingers into the bowl. Paint drips off his fingertips as he pulls them from the bowl then touches them to the corner of Ciquenackqua's eyes. He lets them stray down the young brave's cheeks giving the impression Ciquenackqua weeps streams of blood.

Creek Jumper approaches me next.

His hand and voice shakes with fervor as he dips his fingers anew then raises them to my temple. He drags three fingers across my eyes and bridge of my nose, slathering a red-painted mask across them whilst continuing the ancient war song.

I open my eyes when Creek Jumper beats the drum.

Mercy stares at me from her tied position, her eyes rounding at the sight of Ciquenackqua and me. So, too, do I notice George and Hannah surprised at the doorstep of their cabin, and Mary behind them.

The drum calls me to move, to make the war dance.

I close my eyes again, let my head rock back, and allow my body to shift in blissful sway to the tune of Creek Jumper's voice rising and falling in time with the drum.

Fetching my tomahawk and Father's dagger free from my belt, I add my voice to Creek Jumper's and begin the dance. I twist and spin around the fire, warding off evil spirits with my weapons and voice.

Ciquenackqua joins me in the dance, his movements yet stilted, but freer and with no regard for how he appears.

We dance around the fire, my body never tiring. My thoughts dwell on Sarah, Sturdy Oak, and Deep River, and all the others killed by Mercy and her minions. Memories of Father dragged away bid me dance faster. I scream war cries, giving my loss and sorrow a voice for the first time. Power radiates through me, and I open my eyes to stare on Mercy to let her know the face of death that she might fear it.

Instead, I find her grinning back at me, as if I am a child that pretends at the war dance.

I raise my tomahawk and sling it at the pole, watching the blade buried near her ear.

She flinches at the sound, a sight I relish as I dance near her and pluck it free again.

Ciquenackqua halts near our shaman, raising his dagger high.

"I am Ciquenackqua—"

"No," I cry to him.

His arm drops to his side and he looks on me with concern as I approach.

"No," I say. "We make no claims or boasts this eve. Tonight we avenge those stolen from us and allow any who live to sing our—"

A chunk of wood from Mercy's post explodes in shards.

I wince at the echo of a rifle blast and wheel toward the shooter.

"That were a warnin' shot," Bishop yells. "Take another step and I send yer queen bitch back to Hell, ye powder-snortin' harpies!"

He drops the already fired rifle and raises his second one. As he marches closer to us, I glance over my shoulder to where he focuses. I find the answer beyond the barn.

A group of hooded women, clutching naked blades—hand scythes, daggers, and tomahawks—head toward us.

"Let ye call out to 'em, wench," says Bishop to Mercy. "Call 'em off."

The witches approach us slowly, unafraid.

"Over there," Ciquenackqua shouts. He points to the other end of the yard, toward Bishop's cabin, where a second band of witches makes their presence known.

Indeed, I almost think there are others hidden in the shadows at every corner of the yard, all of them waiting for us to fire or for a word from their mistress.

I look to Mercy and find her smiling.

"Call 'em off." Bishop insists.

"I would hear her swear again," says Mercy to me.

I approach her at the pole and put my dagger to her throat. "Mine are not the words that need proving, witch. You are a liar born of Salem evil. Let you prove yours to me now. Call them off and send them to slay our common enemy, or die with me here now."

"No. I am not so ready to leave this world yet." She looks past me and shouts, "Wait! It is I, Mercy Lewis."

I keep my blade close to Mercy as a single witch steps forward from the others, her face scabbed and picked at, her teeth black and rotted.

"Mistress," she calls. "Give us the word. Let us make short work of these here."

"No," says Mercy. "Not yet. Let you send scouts to the wilderness. Two Ravens comes to this place soon. Let him know I am here and swear over your allegiance in order to see me freed. When the time is right and they bring battle to this post, fall upon his men and slay them."

"But what of you, mistress?" the witch asks. "What of your life?"

Mercy looks on me. "I shall be well protected here, and I would not see my master's prizes tainted or taken from me." She glances back to the witch. "Now go, before Two Ravens arrives and sniffs out our ruse."

The witch groups fades back into darkness, slipping out of sight but not from my mind. I wait awhile, my gaze searching the surrounding cabins for any treacherous sign.

"Ciquenackqua," I say finally. "Get you to the barn with Creek Jumper and hold it. Keep a weather eye on the riverbank."

He nods in reply. As the pair of them makes off for their post, I find myself praying Ciquenackqua's bravery will stand

and that his father's spirit will find its way into him when we fall under attack.

"Bishop," I say. "Do you have your aim on her?"

"Aye, lass. Cut her loose, and let's be off."

I free Mercy from the pole and shove her forward.

"Think on how you treat me now," she says. "I will repay it later down the road."

I pay her no mind, instead whistling toward George's cabin.

Mary hesitates in the entryway, and ultimately runs for me with Hannah's urging.

"You hold the trade cabin with Andrew," I tell her. "Shoot when you can, or else ensure his rifles remain loaded."

"A-aye," she says.

She near stumbles over herself as she leaves me.

No small part of me wonders if my prayers would have been better served on her than Ciquenackqua. Bishop gives me little time to think on it, urging me follow him and Mercy back to his cabin. I bar the door once inside.

The Wyandot brave sits near the hearth, bound and gagged. His eyes follow me warily as I cross the room and grab Mercy by the arm, leading her to the opposite corner.

"It will not be long now," she says.

I bind her wrists and ankles together, much the same as I saw her people do to Sturdy Oak. She winces as I tighten the bonds, but she does not cry out.

Bishop moves about behind us, and I glance over my shoulder in time to see him sit heavily in his chair by the fire. He wheezes and coughs, doubling over as his body racks him. He spits into the fire at the last, and breathes hard, as if the ordeal winded him after a long sprint.

"He is dying," says Mercy.

"No, he's not," I whisper back.

"He is. Many a night I have heard those in Boston cough with the lung sickness." She motions her heard toward Bishop. "He has the same."

"She's right, lass," Bishop says, drawing my attention. "Lying wench that she is, she speaks true now."

I go to him, sitting in the chair he carved special for me. The same chair I sat in as a girl and listened to the tales of his homeland, the place of leprechauns, harpies, and selkies.

"When did you learn of this?" I ask.

"Doesn't matter when I learned it, does it? Can't change it." He fights back another cough. "In truth, I'll soon be damned glad to have done with it all. A tiresome sickness, this."

He grins as he looks on Mercy.

"Ah, but I'll have me one final fight before the end." He pats the rifle in his lap. "Won't we, love?"

He laughs himself into a grievous fit, one leaving his face purple by the end.

"Will you have some water?" I ask.

"Bah," he says. "Give me whiskey, will ye? Let it burn its way through me."

I oblige and watch him drink it down. He spits half of it back out in another consumptive episode. Wincing, he rubs the phlegm remains from his beard. "I fear the banshee draws near."

"If you hear her song," I say, "tell her I would keep you a little longer still."

Bishop grins as he pats my hand. "And I'll demand that wailin' wench take only me."

I chuckle at that, happy to share my time with him, sick though he may be.

"Get some sleep," I tell him. "I will take the watch."

"I'll not have that," he says. "Who's to say ye won't wake me when the fighting begins?"

"I will wake you," I say. "And be glad for your aim."

He winks at me as I rise and carry my chair to sit by Mercy's side, not desiring her company, only ensuring I can cut her throat if our defenses fail.

I take my seat next to the window. My gaze focuses through the small openings left me by the boards across the windows. Though there be little to see but dark and wilderness, I remind myself any manner of scout may be just beyond the tree line, skulking nearer as I should do if making an attack.

"I hate cabins," says Mercy, looking around Bishop's home. "The smell and dark of them. We should have kept outside. At least there we could run, if need be. Here we are trapped."

I snort. "You would have me go outside that your witches could shoot me dead and rescue you?"

"No," she says. "Only so Two Ravens will not burn us alive. There be one escape in here. Only through the door, now that you've boarded the windows. No doubt Two Ravens and his braves will wait there to greet us with their blades." Mercy sighs. "At least we should die of the smoke before the flames reach us."

"You need not worry about flames or smoke," I say.

Mercy grins at my meaning. "Good. If the time comes, see your dagger to my throat quickly. I have witnessed and heard others burned. Their screams still haunt me, aye, but more so their smell. Once you've known the stench of burning flesh, you never forget it. There be many a time I thought to cut off my nose and learn if it would rid me of the memory."

"You should have," I say.

"Perhaps. But then what man would have me?"

"I find it hard to know men would have you now," I say.

"Oh, but they do." She chuckles. "Travel to whatever lands you will, girl. If there be men there, you will find one who would have you, noseless or no. Indeed, some of our people in the colonies tell stories of native men who would enjoy a noseless woman. They who believe natives are the Devil's minions, that is."

Mercy snorts as she rests her head back against the cabin wall.

"But they understand little beyond their borders," she says. "How could they know the Devil walks among them every day in different forms?"

"What do you mean?"

"Men," she says. "Of all colors, shapes, and sizes. They are the Devil's true minions, and they think of us as their prey." Mercy looks to me. "You asked me of Cotton Mather, and why I should follow him?"

"Aye."

"He sent an angel to me. Your father, Dr. Campbell."

"My father—"

"Oh, damn it, girl, think what you will of him. It seems you and I did not know the same man." Mercy says. "Let others say his true purpose were greed, or gain, for both are right. But Dr. Campbell were also the one to give we prey our claws. Aye, teeth to bite the hands that fed us if only we accepted their loathsome offers and starved us when we did not."

"Yet Putnam wrote you lied against women also," I say.

"Aye. You would think our lot in life should bond we women together. Instead we allow men to divide us," says Mercy, her voice rigid and cold. "The women in Salem despised me, shamed me for doing what I must to stay alive. But they never knew suffering like we servant girls. Aye, and those goodly women looked the other way when their husbands came for us in the night."

"Perhaps they deserved death," I say. "But if so, you should have killed them outright rather than lie."

"Sometimes lies are all you have, girl," says Mercy. "You will do well to learn that when we go to Boston. Truths come easy in the wilderness. The savages know nothing of lies and manipulation...but they are learning our ways. Look you no further than Two Ravens if you would know my words true."

I grit my teeth at her words. "You spoke of men looking on you as an animal, yet you speak the same of the natives. Near all of these people are good at heart."

"Let you admire their goodness, if you will, but know that will be the end of them." Mercy exhales. "Not in my lifetime, perhaps, nor even yours, but some day our kind will take these lands from them."

"I am not your kind."

I glance out the window, believing I witness movement near the tree line. A deer moves past a moment later. I release the breath I held and feel my body relax as Mercy continues, almost as if she did not know I paid her little mind.

"No, their kind only now learns the benefits of lying, babes fumbling with a new toy." She scoffs. "But our people are well practiced in the art, and none more than Cotton. He molds this New World to his whims and our people have never felt their strings pulled."

I look on her with disdain. "How do you know your strings are not pulled now?"

"I warrant he does move me," Mercy says. "And it may be Cotton sent me out to have my strings cut. But if so, it were a better life he gave me than the one I had before. People will speak my name long after I am gone because of him. Your father assured us of that."

"I hope they remember you plain," I say. "A lying whore who would betray anyone should the need suit her."

"Perhaps they will," she says. "It matters little to me. I will yet be remembered. Who will know the name Rebecca Kelly? Hmm? None. Cotton will have you and your family wiped from the histories."

"I do not wish to be remembered."

"Liar," says Mercy. "Everyone desires to be remembered by those who follow after, even if painted in a wrongful light. I were but an orphaned girl given to servitude. Who should have thought I would help craft a new nation?"

I laugh at her claim. "You have supped on your Devil's powder too often, if you believe that."

"No," she says. "I never felt the need to see spirits, or learn who my husband should be in the Venus glass, like some of my Salem sisters. I sought only truth and were shown it through the plans of your father and Cotton."

She clucks her tongue. "You laugh at my claims and my wont for a legacy. But one day you shall think back on this night, Rebecca Kelly, and even if all other people from this day till the end of time think of me only as a lying whore, you will know I were the only one to speak truth."

"When I think of you, it will be twofold—the first as my

sister's murderer." I seethe even as I speak the words. "The other of the day I take your life in repayment. Now keep your tongue quiet. I will hear no more from you, lie or otherwise."

She licks her lips. "May I say but one more thing?"

My nostrils flare at her questions. A part of me would tell her no, and slap her that she might understand I spoke truth to her. Still, my curious nature would know what final words she has for me.

"Speak it now," I say. "And be quick with it."

"You wrestle with the truth of my words," says Mercy. "A goodly sign if ever I saw one."

"You speak riddles, witch."

"No. Only truth," says Mercy. "This world is not the one you knew before, but you are adapting, Rebecca. If you survive this night, it may be you learn that which I did when I were near your age."

"And what is that?"

"You can shape it." Mercy grins. "For better or worse."

-seventeen-

ALL NIGHT I KEEP WATCH THROUGH THE SMALL CRACK. MY GAZE never wavers, even as Mercy snores.

Bishop, too, sleeps, his breath raspy and deep like a bear's grumbling.

I rub my eyes, slap myself awake. I lean closer to the window, peering out, and note the night no longer holds its darkest sway, it giving way to hints of purple dawning in the east. Even in dark, a white carpet of ice tinges the grass blades.

Though the hearth fire has long since burned out, I give thanks at least the cabin logs shelter me with some of its former warmth.

I yawn upon leaning back, wonder if Mercy lied about Two Ravens to bide herself time. The sound of wood slapping wood wakes me quick.

A rifle barks, its sound hailing from Andrew and Mary's position.

"Away with ye, ye bleedin' harpies." Bishop shouts behind me. He rises and his bearskin cover falls to the floor. Madness clouds his eyes as he brings his rifle to the ready, searching for the sound's origin.

I grab up my own rifle, knocking over my chair as I run to the northwestern window for a better view.

"What was that, lass?" Bishop asks. "Do they come?"

"I know not."

I squint out the window crack, and see Andrew stumble off the trade cabin porch, falling flat on his face.

"Oh no..." I say.

"George," Andrew cries as he fumbles to find his feet. "George, I'm sorry."

"Who's that then?" Bishop asks.

"Andrew..." I say, as he wobbles in the middle of the yard, planting his rifle and using it to steady himself. "He's drunk."

"George..." Andrew yells again. "Come out here and talk to me!"

I lean closer to the window when Andrew near falls over again, catching himself at the last.

"Andrew! Get back to your post."

"George." Andrew covers his face with his hands. "George, no. No, I must speak with you now."

"We'll speak later," George thunders. "Get back to the cabin."

I pray to the ancestors that Andrew listens. My prayer goes unheeded.

"You don't understand," Andrew slurs as he drops to the ground. "It's all my fault, George...Everything."

"Andrew—"

"No! It's all my fault." Andrew puts his face in the earth, rocks back and forth.

"What's he doin' then?" Bishop asks.

I shake my head, my tongue not forming the words as my brother runs to Andrew's side.

"Get up, Andrew." George pulls him to his feet.

"G-George, I'm s-sorry."

"Enough with you." George flings Andrew back toward the cabin. "I said—"

A rifle barks.

My brother's shoulder jerks back, spinning him. He falls to earth.

"No!"

My scream matches Andrew's.

He falls upon George, grabbing my brother under his arms, and trips himself as he attempts to pull George toward the trade cabin.

More shots ring out in quick succession, this time from the northeast—George and Hannah's cabin.

The whoops and war cries of braves, and the furious screeching of women, ring as one.

"What do ye see, lass?" Bishop asks.

I scarcely know what to say. No sooner does Andrew tug George onto the porch, than I see Mary fleeing. She sprints across the yard as if chased by an evil spirit.

"No…" I stand to the window. "Mary, stop!"

She halts near the middle of the yard, looks my way.

"Stop!" I cry again.

Mary shakes her head. She takes a single look back toward the cabin and my wounded brother. Then she retreats toward the wilderness, abandoning us all.

My mind bids me rise and fling open the door, go to stop her, or else help Andrew with George. I know not what keeps me holding my position, but I am glad of it a moment later when a rifle end pokes through the trade cabin window.

My gut warns George must be alive for the shots from inside come too quick for a lone shooter.

"Rebecca," Mercy cries. "Free me now and give me a rifle. Let me stand with you!"

I do not deign to give her a reply.

The first of the braves comes into my sights. Not a few follow after, all of them with a witch nearby.

Again, Andrew's shots ring out, wounding one of the braves but not felling him.

Still the others keep on, and Mercy's witches too.

"Mercy lied," I say to Bishop. "Her witches march with the braves."

"For now," Mercy says. "What good is a trap if you do not set it well?"

I shake off her words and raise my aim to the window crack.

"There's more headed for yer brother's cabin," says Bishop from the opposite wall.

Fear stabs my heart, my thoughts on Hannah.

"She will be alone now," I say. "Alone without George to fend them off—"

My words go muted when Bishop fires his rifle. The echo near deafens me and a smoky haze fills the cabin. I cough with the others, wave it from my face, and remind myself to focus.

I take a witch in my sights. My finger quivers on the trigger, preparing to squeeze.

The last witch in the train brings down the brave beside her. She stabs him in the back, her dagger falling and rising while the others in their company continue on.

"Shoot the braves." I tell Bishop. "Mercy spoke true. Her witches fight with us!"

I take aim at a brave, shoot and watch him stumble to earth.

He does not rise.

I reach for a new rifle, bring its end to the window, and learn I am too late. Braves have reached the trade cabin. Some bear lit torches. One runs along the side, trying to spark the wood. Others heave their torches upon the roof.

Seeing the fire catch, I fell another brave with my shot then reach for the third and final rifle. I take careful aim, resting the rifle end just outside the window.

It is jerked from my grasp in an instant, its butt shoved back at my face.

My reaction to fall backward saves my nose and forehead, though it costs me my position.

A painted brave appear in the window. He peers through the boarded cracks. Whoops a war cry. Then he gasps, his face falling from my sight.

The black hood of a witch briefly appears in its place and then vanishes.

Women scream, though some of their cries have changed. No longer are all victorious or full of rage. Now some sound pained.

"They have learned our trap," Mercy calls to me. "Free me that I might help! Now, before it is too late."

The sounds do not quit, and I look to the spent rifles by the window.

A window board is knocked loose and a torch thrown inside, rolling near our Wyandot hostage. He shouts at me in unknown words, though their meaning is plain and well taken.

I run to his side and pluck up the torch, throw it inside the hearth to burn out.

"Bishop," I say.

"Aye, lass?"

"Hold the cabin."

"Aye," he shouts. "That I will. Now do yer grandpappy proud, lass. Fetch me some witches."

I look on the now open window, pull my tomahawk and Father's dagger free from my belt. I throw myself against the wall, waiting for the torch thrower to peek inside.

A brave leans in to look a moment later.

I show the tip of Father's dagger through his eye, running it to the hilt before shoving him off it. I back away from the window then take a deep breath and sprint for it. Diving through the opening, I roll the moment I land upon the cold, slick earth and bring my blades to the ready.

Chaos surrounds me.

Witches fight braves, some of them ganging up to fell their stronger opponents. Others are singled out and tossed aside to die screeching at the hands of the native braves.

A war cry rises behind me.

I duck at the blade whistling above my head. I stab Father's dagger backward, raising it up and twisting. Listen to my attacker's gurgle. Yanking my dagger free, I search the outside the cabin for any more attackers.

Then I see George and Hannah's house aflame.

I sprint toward it, rolling beneath another brave come to slay me. I trip him up by slicing his ankle, then swing my tomahawk upon his chest to end him.

Again, I find my feet. My mind reels from the noise, not just of battle, but the animals from the barn. Father's stallion rears and kicks at its wooden confines, as if it too wishes to join our fight.

The barn itself blazes, no doubt catching faster from the straw and hay inside.

Creek Jumper stands just beyond the barn. He surprises me with his quick and easy ways, swinging his own tomahawk as if he were a brave no older than twenty.

Ciquenackqua stands beside him. Though he does not move in the same manner as his elder, the pair move in tandem, wreaking havoc on any who dare cross them.

The popping of burning wood calls my attention back to my brother's home. The door hangs off its hinges with traces of smoke escaping through the opening.

I think of Hannah, and then rush inside. Dropping to my chest, crawling forward as smoke clouds my nostrils and blinds my eyes.

"Hannah..." I cry. "Hannah, where are you?"

I cannot tell whether she replies, or else I am deaf to all sound.

Heat swarms me, choking the life from my lungs.

I use my hands in swinging arcs, praying I find no purchase as I search the kitchen and move onto the back wall. My forearm grazes flesh and my heart near stops when brushing Hannah's ankle. I use her leg to guide me up and touch my fingers to her neck.

She has no pulse.

I cough at the smoke filling my lungs. My body begs me leave this hellish place or else surrender to the black spots popping in my vision.

I lean my back against the wall, raise my arms above my head, and feel for the windowsill. I rap my knuckles against it, feel the window barred.

I scoot further down the wall, continuing my search until my fists hit naught but air.

Then I return to Hannah's body, grabbing her by the arm and dragging her closer to the open window. I steady my feet beneath me and try to lift her.

My body fails me, her weight too heavy for me.

I think of she and George's tender moment when last I saw them together.

The memory gifts me new strength.

Moving behind Hannah, I push her forward, inching us across the kitchen floor. I risk opening my eyes and wince at the hints of light.

Smoke saps what little strength I have left.

My body warns it will not last much longer. I scream at the pain and shove Hannah forward.

It is enough to reach the door.

I fall outside and off the porch, pulling Hannah's weight atop me. My chest heaves for fresh air, and that I suck in greedily.

New life flutters in me with each breath drawn, and I will myself to see how my companions fare.

Only a handful of braves yet stand, and those surrounded by witches with bloodied long daggers.

A pair of braves notices Hannah and me upon the ground. Screaming, they rush me.

A rifle barks and the first brave falls.

The death of his ally causes the second brave to pause.

I look to learn my savior.

George stands upon the trade cabin porch, bringing a new rifle to aim even as his shoulder bleeds. He shoots the second brave dead without thought. His gaze slides from me to his wife, and then he runs across the yard, leaping over the dead and dying. He falls beside me and rolls Hannah onto her back.

"Hannah," he says. "Speak to me, wife."

He takes hold of her soot-covered face in his grimy hands, raises her to sit with him.

Hannah's head lolls upon his shoulder, her glazed eyes staring in fearless question into the morning sun.

"*Hannah!*" George cries, his voice breaking like a wounded animal as he clutches her close. He rocks back and forth, sucking air. "No, no, no...Hannah...Oh, Hannah..."

My spirit speaks to me that hers has already left this world. Tears sting my eyes.

The clashing of blades calls me from mourning.

I look to the origin of its sound and there see a lone brave yet standing, felling Mercy's witches with the war club he stole from Whistling Hare.

Two Ravens slays the last of his attackers. He looks for any more opponents and sneers upon noticing me.

My strength returns quick enough. My knuckles whiten at the grip I form around the hilt of Father's dagger. I take my tomahawk also, rising to my feet and hurrying to meet Two Ravens in the yard.

Neither of us hesitates in our course as we close on one another.

He swoops the war club wide.

I dive to miss it, following Father's example to chip away at my opponent with smaller cuts rather than risk a finishing blow as Two Ravens would.

"You killed my brother," he says upon facing me.

"Aye," I say. "And would again."

He lunges forward, swinging the war club down toward my skull.

I miss the attempt easy enough, but he surprises me with a second blow.

The strength of his fist grazing my cheek rattles my brain and causes me to stumble.

Two Ravens laughs.

My sight dizzy, two of him approach me though I cannot rightly determine which one is real and the other his shade.

He kicks my stomach, finishing the job his fist did not. It steals the wind from me, leaving me gasping, crawling upon the ground.

"What hope did you have to defeat me, woman?" he asks. "I told Mercy you were weak. Now you will die for it."

He raises his war club to end me.

A shadow knocks him down.

Two Ravens falls beside me with Ciquenackqua atop him, the younger brave plunging his dagger into the seasoned warrior like chipping a hunk of ice free of the river.

Ciquenackqua rolls away, and me with him, before Two Ravens might land his hands upon us.

Two Ravens struggles to his knees, his breath labored and wheezing.

"Look at me." Ciquenackqua holds his father's war club.

But he spoke the command not to me, his gaze homed on Two Ravens.

"Who are you, boy?" Two Ravens asks. "That you would kill Two Ravens like a woman? Attacking from behind."

"I am Ciquenackqua, son of Whistling Hare, and you die at my hands today." He looks on the war club. "And by my father's weapon."

Two Ravens laughs. "You don't have the stomach for it. I saw you run—"

Ciquenackqua swings the war club with such precision that he near cleaves the head of Two Ravens.

The man who took my father falls to earth, his skull caved in, near the same as it were done to Sturdy Oak.

Ciquenackqua drops the war club and takes a knee. His shoulders trembling and breath panicked for air.

I think to go to him when another rifle barks.

My sight swivels in search of the sound. There be no witch or brave left alive, though dead aplenty.

As for my own people, Creek Jumper limps toward us. Blood streaks his chest and face, though whether it be his own or that of his enemies I cannot be certain.

George yet holds Hannah in his arms, rocking as I left him earlier.

Then I look to the trade cabin.

Andrew sits upon the porch, his arm bleeding, eyes lost in a fog of war, and his head leaning upon a post as the cabin blazes behind him.

My sight falls on Bishop's cabin, and the kicked-in door.

Fear grabs hold of me at the memory I left through the window.

Inside, a hooded figure moves from one side of the cabin to the other.

I am on my feet and sprinting without thought to what lay inside.

A witch greets me the moment I enter.

I fell her easy enough with a slash of Father's dagger, ending her with the tomahawk.

It is the witch standing beside Bishop's table that halts me.

The one with her knife buried in his gut.

"Lass..." Bishop wheezes, coughs up blood. "Kill this bitch for me."

Then she shoves him backward, tipping his chair to crash upon the cabin floor, pulling her crimson-coated blade free.

Mercy grins at me. "Shall we dance again, white squaw?"

I FLY AT MERCY, SCREAMING CURSES, RAINING BLOW AFTER BLOW upon her.

She meets them with her own, knocking mine astray or else dodging them.

The few cuts I connect with and the pain escaping her lips fuel me, as do the few blows she gifts me back. Each of them fills me with rage.

"I told you to kill me when you had the chance," says Mercy.

I rush her anew, our blades singing upon one another until she again kicks me back.

"I lent you my witches to fight," she says. "And this is how you repay me? You are a traitor to your vows, girl, just like that scheming coward Mary Warren."

The mention infuriates me. I duck beneath Mercy's swing, and catch my tomahawk to her ankle, jerking up and slicing her tendon.

"Ahh!" Mercy yelps, falling to her knee.

I kick her in the back but do not move to end her.

"Get up," I bid, relishing her pain.

Mercy flies to her feet. She swings her blades, slicing an inch from my nose, missing.

I butt my head into hers and watch her stumble back.

Dropping to my knee, I whirl my tomahawk and catch her other ankle. I jerk up and hear her scream as the edge cuts her other tendon.

Mercy growls on the floor, dropping her blades and feeling for her ankles.

"Get up," I say.

"Are you soft in the head, girl?" she asks, panting for breath.

"Get up."

"No," says Mercy. "I think I'll lie here and wait for you to kill me—"

"Get...up..."

"Just like your cripple sister."

My mind goes blank, my vision blazing red.

When my sight returns, I find Mercy's blood and mine soaks the pair of us so that I cannot discern which of us suffers the greater wounds. Her howls tell me she bears the brunt of them.

"Kill me..." she begs. "K-kill me now."

I shut out her pleas, thinking of how she turned a deaf ear to Sarah.

Movement in the corner draws my attention—the Wyandot hostage watching me. He shrinks as I rise from Mercy, blood staining my arms and neck, and step closer to both the tipped chair and Bishop's body.

The old man's eyes flicker as I kneel beside him, taking his head in my lap.

"Are ye the banshee?" Bishop asks. "Come to sing me home at long last?"

Tears drip down my cheeks as the singsong tone I well remember in his storytelling has gone, replaced by a voice weak and faded. I look on his wounds, and see his breaths slowing, each one taken with great effort.

"No," I say. "It is I, your favorite...Rebecca. Remember?"

"Rebecca?" He blinks. "I-I don't…Augh. Aye…I remember now. Did ye hide the wee poppets, lass?"

I cry harder at the realization of his words, thinking he must remember me now as the little girl I was, one scared of the attacks that would come. I recall how he put aside my fears with his gentle voice and once assigned me the simple task of hiding my poppets to occupy my mind.

"Did ye…did ye keep them safe, then?"

"No," I say, thinking of Sarah and Sturdy Oak, Hannah and Numees, even Father. "I-I could not keep them safe."

"It's all right, dear." Bishop pats my hand. "We'll find a place…a place for them. Don't ye worry now…Pr-Priest will help ye."

His mention of Father's name bids me cry harder.

"He is gone, Grandfather," I say through my tears. "Th-they took him too."

"Don't worry, lass…he'll be back," says Bishop. "Good lad, him. Even if he is a…mouthy bastard. Always comes back, he does."

He trembles in my arms.

"I'm cold, dear," he says. "So very cold."

I leave his side and find his bearskin, lay it gently over his body up to his shoulders.

Bishop smiles at my touch and his gaze wanders before settling upon my face. "Are ye the banshee?"

I rest my forehead upon his, my body racked with pain, my spirit breaking.

"Come to sing me home at long last?" Bishop asks.

I pull away, knowing what I must do.

"A-aye," I say, stroking his hair. "I am the banshee."

He grunts. "Funny, that…thought ye'd be older. Ugly. Instead ye…ye look like me favorite granddaughter…R-Rebecca."

"Do I?" I sputter the words.

"Aye," he says. "Will ye grant me one last wish, love?"

"Any—anything."

"Sing," he says. "Sing me to sleep. Then take me home… I'd have me a pint with St. Peter…and see me poor Annie again."

My mind struggles to think of a song. I stare into his grizzled face, and sing the one I know best. The one he sang to me many a night when I would cry out for my mother and father, frightened that Hecate and her witches would come take me also. I open my mouth, and then begin his song.

Come, fair lass, just you and me.
We're bound for them colonies, far o'er the sea…

"Aye, sing," he says softly, his head nodding. "Just sing…"

I wet my cracked lips and continue, though my throat runs dry.

'Augh, no,' she said. 'You stubborn old fool.
I've heard of those lands, and them savages cruel.'
So the Lord took pity and sent me some cheer,
Reb—

My voice quavers, and I fight to continue his lullaby.

Rebecca's her name, the pretty little dear.
'Come, lass,' says I. 'Let you not fear no witches.'
Your grandpappy's here—

His head dozes upon my arm as he breathes his last breath.

My tears fall upon his brow, my voice catching in my throat.

And he'll kill them bitches.

I collapse upon Bishop, my chest heaving as I take in his

smell, willing him hold me one last time, knowing it can never be again.

Mercy groans upon the floor. "Kill me…"

I do not stir from Bishop and cannot rightly guess how long I sit with him, only that I recognize my body and soul numb when the sound of footsteps crosses upon the porch.

Ciquenackqua's face turns ashen seeing me with Bishop. "Rebecca, I…"

"Leave me…"

"We are surrounded."

I glance up and, seeing Ciquenackqua serious, I lay Bishop's head gently upon the floor and leave his side to learn the truth of Ciquenackqua's words. Stepping over Mercy's hand that reaches out for me, I peek out the open door.

Near a hundred native braves encircle the trade post, all of them armed.

My mind warns I should be afeared at such a sight.

I sweep the thought aside with numbness, leaving Ciquenackqua to stand upon the porch as I reenter the cabin. I look on Mercy, then to Bishop, and finally on the Wyandot hostage. The ringed-tail tattoo upon his chest draws my attention, turning my thoughts to my *manitous* and the path it has led me down.

"Rebecca—"

I point to the Wyandot hostage. "Bring him outside, Ciquenackqua."

I kneel beside Mercy, grip her hair in my hand and jerk on it that she might look up and know me.

"Do it," she says. "Kill me."

I stare into her eyes and, at long last, I understand the silence with which Father shields himself. Knowing now he wears the mask not out of mourning, but hate. Strong enough it needs no words to convey.

I yank Mercy to her feet, and lead her out, forcing her on even when her wounds stumble her.

"Come," I say to her, my voice steady and cold. "I will not be slowed by a cripple."

"Rebecca, wait," she says.

The sight of George yet clutching Hannah's body bids me hasten Mercy along faster.

I lead her to the middle of the yard where Creek Jumper stands, watching the braves around us. He squints in wonder as Ciquenackqua and I lead our hostages toward him, halting together that all might witness.

"You don't know...what you're doing," says Mercy. "Hear me, Rebecca. I—"

"Are those your people?" I ask the Wyandot hostage, pointing to the braves around us.

Creek Jumper repeats my words in the foreign tongue.

I need not hear the hostage's reply to understand my assumption right.

"The Wyandot are not our enemy," I say, raising my voice loud for all to hear. "Nor are the Iroquois. My enemy is the white devil in Boston, the Reverend Cotton Mather. He who sent this woman and her kind to kill my family."

Creek Jumper repeats my words in their tongue, and the braves look upon one another when he finishes.

I cut the Wyandot brave free of his bonds, then push him away.

He looks on me oddly, as if suspecting a trick.

Instead, I face those surrounding us.

"We give this man back to you. Let him speak the truth of my claims, for I would not war against you this day." My voice rises as I walk to Mercy. "But I will slaughter any who comes against my family!"

I kick Mercy to her knees. My fingers close tighter around her hair, my nails digging deep in her scalp. I yank her head back and look down into her eyes, bringing the edge of Father's dagger to her forehead.

"A kindred spirit indeed." Mercy spits the words, her eyes wild and defiant as they stare up into mine.

I glance up at the Wyandot warriors. Feel them watching me, waiting.

"No." I stay my hand, though feeling the blade hesitate upon her scalp. "I am not like you, not a savage, nor butcher of innocents. I am of the people."

"Your people are weak," she says. "And will be wiped from the histories."

"Perhaps," I say. "But you will never see it."

I lower my dagger to her throat, and feel her tremble.

"Rebecca, no—"

I scream her quiet, shutting my ears and senses to Mercy and everything around me. I live in my pain and lose myself to the blood lust and hate for all who took those I held dear.

When my senses return, Mercy lies dead at my feet.

I look to the braves, and observe not a few nervous glances among them.

"I am the daughter of Black Pilgrim!" I shriek at them. "And I do not fear. Let you learn the strength of my spirit."

I issue a war cry, long and sharp, meeting their stares, my gaze unwavering.

"Come for me." I wave Father's dagger at them. "Come and learn well what befalls those who cross us. Or befriend us now and let me end this white devil who plagues us!"

The hostage we released returns to his people. My blood no longer runs hot at the idea of a fight. Emptiness engulfs me.

"What should we do if they come down on us?" Ciquenackqua asks.

I look on him blankly. "We die."

I stand by my companions and wait.

But the Wyandot do not come upon us.

Instead, they slip away, back into the wilderness, disappearing.

"Do they mean to trick us?" Ciquenackqua asks. "Where are they going?"

Creek Jumper steps forward, the bones in his necklace rattling. "They find us worthy of life."

"No," I say. "They know us already dead inside."

I leave my companions, and walk to Mercy's body. As I look into her eyes, I will the hate in me to return, the desire to mangle her body further.

Nothing rises in me. Nothing stirs.

Not until my ears prick at the sound of women's voices, coming from the woods.

I hesitate, swearing someone calls my name.

"Who is that?" Ciquenackqua asks.

A native woman runs from the wilderness toward us, her raven hair streaming behind her.

"Numees..." I say.

I sprint toward her, noticing others follow her from the woods. Women and children, a few of Ciquenackqua's younger friends, and all familiar faces.

I beat both Ciquenackqua and Creek Jumper to the survivors of our village.

Numees and I crash into one another, embracing, weeping, touching each other's faces as if we both doubt the other real.

Ciquenackqua runs past us, lifting his mother off her feet as he reaches her. He twirls her around and cries as he sets her gently back to earth.

"Mother," he says. "Mother, Father is—"

"You are alive, my son," she shushes him. "That is all that matters now."

Creek Jumper kisses his wife. She touches his wounds, her face pained at the sight of them. He merely shakes his head and draws her close.

"Rebecca," says Numees. "I thought to never see you again."

"And I you."

I embrace her again. I look around those from my village, searching for one other face and not finding him.

"Numees," I say. "Wh-where is my father?"

Her hesitation stabs at my heart.

"After learning of your escape, Two Ravens and his men dragged your father to the river." She shakes her head. "Two Ravens returned—"

I wilt in her arms, falling to my knees.

"Your father did not."

My body heaves at her words, and I feel her presence beside me, comforting me with her hand upon my back.

I shrug it off, all my happiness at seeing her and the others alive stolen in an instant.

I climb to my feet and return to Bishop's cabin alone. I shut my eyes to the remains of Mercy's bindings upon the floor and the wrecked household, my focus drawn upon the man who told stories to make me laugh and learned me that I was safe in his presence.

I lie beside Bishop and wrap his arm about me. Then I weep as I have never done before. I clutch his limp hand, wish it would squeeze mine back and comfort me one last time.

But he is gone.

And he would be cross with me for wailing at the loss of him and Father. I know he would instead bid me rise up and take my vengeance upon those who hurt the ones I love, rather than submit to grief as Sarah did.

But Bishop says nothing.

And I have not his strength, nor can I bear the thought of giving he and the others up yet. Instead, I fall asleep at his side, dreaming of happier times.

I wake to afternoon and reality.

"Rebecca."

I look to the doorway and see Creek Jumper.

"Come," he says. "We must help him down the spirit path now."

"No," I say, looking on Bishop's grizzled and scarred face. "He would not wish us bury him, nor us abandon him upon a rack for the crows to pick at."

"Then what?"

"We will burn him." I say. "That his spirit might fly home and look on it one last time. Then I will bear his ashes away."

-nineteen-

DUSK SETTLES IN AS I WANDER AWAY FROM THE TRADE POST AND down toward the river.

I pass through the opening once separating George's barn from the trade cabin. Now there be little of both. Glancing back, I see even his and Hannah's cabin smoldering, a blackened husk of the bright home I remember it being.

An east wind blows smoke and the scent of death toward me where a mound of witches and braves yet burns as Ciquenackqua and Andrew throw the remaining corpses into its flames. Andrew catches me watching and hangs his head, shows me his back.

I struggle with my feelings. Not knowing whether to hate him for his earlier actions, or be thankful at least he yet lives with so many others dead. I decide not to dwell on such thoughts, turning my attention instead to the Wah-Bah-Shik-Ka and the lone figure seated upon its banks.

The memory of George carrying Hannah's body away from their home remains fixed in my mind, how my brother walked past me as if none of us existed in the world.

George sits now beside a fresh mound of dirt, its top smoothed over, and bearing a wooden cross at its head. He does not even glance over his shoulder as I approach, his gaze on the setting sun.

I sit cross-legged next to him, listening to the tireless river flow, and losing myself to its dispassionate thought of our grief.

We sit together in silence as the sky turns purple. My thoughts dwell on Father again, and the value in such a quiet manner. I find it comforting at such times as now when no words can right the wrongs, nor heal any wounds. That being present alone suffices.

"Thank you," says George finally. "For saving her."

"I am only sorry I did not reach her earlier."

"It is enough you rescued her body from the fire."

My brother's chin drops, his cheeks glistening with the final rays of day.

"Strange," George says. "Hannah and I would lie out here many a day and night, looking up at the sky. Talking of nothing, or our children to come, or else looking up the river and wondering when we might see your canoes approaching."

He pats the mound beside him.

"I thought it right to place her here," he says. "Here where she might listen to the river while I am away. She ever loved its song."

"Aye," I say. "She often said as much to me when we would fish upon this shore."

George smiles. "I remember a day you pushed her in."

"Aye, and I recall you throwing me in after her for my doing so."

We chuckle at the shared memory before the sadness returns to claim us both.

"I have been long questioning myself if it were wrong of us to think we might escape our father's sins," says George. "And how grievous the acts he committed must have truly been for God to punish our family so."

He wipes his nose and clears his throat.

"Then I realized this be no work of God, nor punishment from Him either." George shakes his head as he looks on Hannah's grave. "This be the evil works of men. I were wrong to think we might escape it and now my dear wife has paid for my mistake."

"If you were wrong," I say, "so were we all."

"Aye. Wrong to believe they would let us alone. They allowed us peace that we might forget them for a time only so it would pain us all the more when stolen again." George looks at me. "But now I would steal it from them, Rebecca."

My mind races with assumptions to his meaning.

"We made a promise to Mercy that we together should go to Boston if surviving the night. I will see that vow carried out now." George's voice drips with hate. "And on my wife's honor, I will not quit until this is ended."

Tears fill my eyes at the conviction in his voice. A call for vengeance and blood stirs within me. "Nor will I."

George puts his arm around me, draws me close.

I lay my head on his shoulder, feel him kiss my brow.

"Do not mistake my grief for the happiness at seeing you yet live, sister," he says. "I should have ended myself also if I had found you among the dead."

"And I you," I say. "We are all that is left now, brother."

"We will be enough."

"Aye," I say. "We shall be."

I look up at the stars, watching them twinkle and make themselves known.

I chuckle at a memory, though George looks on me oddly.

"What?" he asks.

"Bishop told me once that stars were the spirits of good men and women looking down on us, showing us their goodly light. Guiding our way and warding off even the darkest of nights."

"Aye," says George. "I am sure he is one of them now."

"No, he is not." I burst out laughing, an odd sound to draw even a smirk from George. "He told me never to look for him in the night sky after he were dead. That watching and guiding from above sounded a tedious afterlife to him."

"To him, I think it might well have been," says George.

"Aye. He said ghosts had more sport." I laugh anew. "And that I should think of him whenever something bumped in the night."

George joins my laughter, the pair of us wiping our tears away at the notion of Bishop's spirit living on, only to fright us.

My laughter fades as I glance back up the hill, hating the task that remains, knowing I must face it.

"We mean to burn his body," I tell George. "I thought you might wish to join us."

"Aye, I will be along," he says. "Let you go for now though. I would sit alone with my wife a bit longer."

I stand to take my leave of him and send up a silent prayer that the ancestors guide Hannah's goodly spirit and welcome her among them.

Climbing the hill alone, I look on Bishop's funeral pyre built in the middle of the yard.

My people gather around it.

I pause seeing Ciquenackqua and Andrew lift Bishop's bundled body atop it.

Then a tittering hails from what remains of the barn. Walking toward it, I find my father's stallion waiting at the fence line and, sitting atop the post, a raccoon.

The ringed-tail chatters at me, its eyes reflecting the glow of the torches my people hold.

I stare at the black mask painted across its face, thinking on all I have learned. The path it led me down and where it leads me next. More important still, the masks I have yet to learn and which will suit me best.

Turning away from my *manitous,* I find Creek Jumper waits for me near the pyre, holding a lit torch.

I join him in the middle taking hold of the torch and stepping close to the pyre, looking up at Bishop's wrapped body.

"Goodbye, Grandfather," I whisper, allowing the flame to kiss the kindling. "Fly home knowing you are avenged."

The fire catches, and I back away as its flames snake up the four posts, licking Bishop's body, growing in brilliance as it takes full hold of the pyre.

Creek Jumper offers up his voice, singing one of the ancient songs. The others in my tribe add their voices to his.

I keep to Father's quiet way, masking my grief and hate with silence.

Still, I live in the power of their words and the unison of their voices, delighting in the knowledge I am not alone. I know these around me are family also, and will stay at my side all night if I have need of them.

They cease the song of a sudden.

Not a few of our women gasp as part of the circle breaks.

A trio of braves stands on the border of firelight and darkness, one an impressive native who leaves little doubt he is their war chief. To his right stands a younger brave I well recognize—the hostage I had in my care. Seeing the two side by side, I think it easy to know them for father and son.

The third brave holds his own hostage. An over-sized woman with her hands bound behind her back and a noose round her neck, its end leading to the rope held in his hand.

"Mary Warren..." I say.

At a foreign word from the war chief, the brave leads Mary toward me. Fear and panic glow in her eyes as they cross the yard. The brave makes a show of handing the rope to me, and his chieftain speaks again.

"He says the debt is paid," says Creek Jumper, stepping to join me. "A captive for you in exchange for the safe return of his son."

"Thank him for me," I say, taking the rope in hand, acknowledging the chieftain as Creek Jumper relays my words.

I stare into Mary Warren's eyes, my hatred burning clear for her, knowing now that Mercy spoke true—Mary is a coward and abandoned us all in our time of greatest need. I realize now she would do again if given half a chance.

She means to speak with me, but the gag in her mouth keeps back her traitorous words.

I think there be little reason to remove the gag and hear them.

The brave returns to his chieftain, and I am not a little surprised when his son, the captive I kept, steps forward next. All while his father continues speaking to us.

"They have thought long on your words," Creek Jumper translates. "And would have peace with Red Banshee and her people."

I turn to Creek Jumper of a sudden. "What did you say?"

He grins as the captive we kept walks toward us, bearing a gift in his hands.

"They knew nothing of your name," says Creek Jumper. "But his son heard Bishop call you banshee and they saw for themselves your spirit and body red with fury."

The young brave stands before me, raises both his hands up to me bearing a *calumet,* a peace pipe of his people that gleams of polished wood in the firelight.

"They offer this token as a sign of peace," says Creek Jumper. "They were given it by the Iroquois as a symbol of the peace they wished to uphold. A peace Two Ravens meant to destroy. We saw to the punishment both peoples would have given him."

I take the *calumet* in hand and nod to the brave in mutual respect as his father continues.

"They will stay tonight, that we might honor our dead," says Creek Jumper. "And they promise safe passage through their lands when you are prepared to leave."

"What of the Iroquois?" I ask. "Will the Wyandot speak to them also and cool their anger?"

Creek Jumper relays my words and keeps careful watch of the Wyandot chieftain. I wonder what he must think of me as he speaks.

"Yes," says Creek Jumper. "They will escort you to the Iroquois lands, telling of your deeds and what you have done for the people. In return, they ask that you hold true to your vow"—Creek Jumper looks on me—"and end this white devil who plagues all our peoples."

Staring into the eyes of the Wyandot chieftain, I grip the *calumet* tight and thrust my hand into the air. Ciquenackqua leads our people in a war cry, and the chieftain's chin dips in acceptance.

I lower my arm, and stare upon the *calumet.* I think of Father's teachings and how he raised me to hunt, rather than hide as we have done for so many years. I rub my fingers over the *calumet* and look up.

Andrew stands before me. Anger rises in me at the sight of him, yet I do nothing.

"You will journey to Boston?" he asks. "Truly?"

"Aye—"

I turn at my brother's voice. George strides toward us.

"And you are coming with us, Andrew."

"George," says Andrew. "I cannot—"

My brother grabs Andrew by the shirt and shakes him.

"My wife died on account of you," George thunders. "She should be here still if not for your drunken way. And your cowardice," he spits at Mary then looks on me. "Throw her to the fire, sister. Let her burn for her sins."

"No," I say. "She comes with us also."

"You cannot trust her," George says.

"Aye, and I do so no longer. But she is a Salem sister," I say, looking Mary Warren in the eye. "And it might be she has some use to us yet."

"As you might also," says George to Andrew. "You said earlier these events were your fault. That your future wife gave our presence away to Mercy Lewis."

"George, I—"

"Do not speak my name as if I am friend or family to you any longer, Andrew Martin," says George. "We are neither from this night on, though I will see you make amends to my family."

"How?" Andrew asks. "Let you name it and I shall do—"

"Lead us to your bride," says George. "For I would have words with her also."

Andrew squirms in George's grip, and yet he looks to me. "Let you speak some sense to your brother, Rebecca."

"No," I say, glancing back to the barn, and seeing my *manitous* gone. "Call me that no longer in the wilderness. That name were only a mask I wore for a time. I am the daughter of Black Pilgrim, and I, too, have a name given me by my native brothers and sisters."

I look into the fiery pyre. Feel its warmth penetrate my skin, liken to the rage burning within me, as I unsheathe the dagger in my belt.

"I am Red Banshee. And before his end, Cotton Mather will hear me sing his name"—I rotate the dagger in the firelight—"and feel my song of fury."

-twenty-

SWELLED BRUISES HELD HOSTAGE THE PRISONER'S EYES, BUT HE could still hear.

He listened to his native captors demand a better price for the sale of him, noted the English dialects on the tongues of those bidding.

They know. The prisoner recognized the strained desire to win him in their voices. *They know of my lineage and my worth.*

With each passing exchange, the prisoner grew more certain the Englishmen would buy him, no matter the price asked by the natives.

From the darkness holding him, the same blackness for which the natives named him, the prisoner called a memory—a face to grant him strength for the journey ahead. A reminder of why he must live.

Then, soft as wind rustling through blades of grass, he spoke her name.

"Rebecca."

Acknowledgments

As a boy, my maternal grandmother told me tales of our forefathers and said the blood of a proud people—the Miamiak—flowed in our veins. God only knows how much time I spent in the woods behind her home pretending I was a brave. Their stories will forever fascinate me, as I hope this story has fascinated you.

In regards to this novel, I could not have done without my coven: Annetta Ribken, Jennifer Wingard, Greg Sidelnik, and Valerie Bellamy. Thank you all for lending me your many talents and knowledge to shape *Salem's Fury*.

To Karen, my wife and first reader, thank you for loving me and believing in me, especially seeing as I don't write kissy-kissy books, provide the endings you hope for, or change the fates of characters even when you demand it.

To my parents, siblings, and the countless family and friends who have followed my crazy antics all this way, my thanks for your continued support.

And thank you, dear reader, for continuing this journey with me.

About the Author

Aaron Galvin runs the creative gamut.

He cut his chops writing stand-up comedy routines at age thirteen. His early works paid off years later when he co-wrote and executive produced the award-winning indie feature film, *Wedding Bells & Shotgun Shells*. In addition to the Vengeance Trilogy, he also authors the Salt series, a YA urban fantasy praised for a unique take on mermaids and selkies.

He is also an accomplished actor. Aaron has worked in everything from Hollywood blockbusters, (Christopher Nolan's *The Dark Knight*, and Clint Eastwood's *Flags of Our Fathers*), to starring in dozens of indie films and commercials.

Aaron is a native Hoosier, graduate of Ball State University, and a proud member of SCBWI. He currently lives in Southern California with his wife and children.

For more information, please visit his website:

www.aarongalvin.com

Made in the USA
Charleston, SC
01 September 2015